Silvertip's Strike

OTHER SILVERTIP ADVENTURES
BY MAX BRAND

Silvertip's Roundup
The Stolen Stallion
Silvertip
Silvertip's Search
The Man from Mustang

Silvertip's Strike

MAX BRAND

A MAX BRAND CLASSIC

**The
Silvertip Adventure
Series**

DODD, MEAD & COMPANY
New York

First published in Western Story Magazine in 1933 under the title
Silver's Strike, and subsequently in book form in 1942 by Dodd,
Mead & Company, Inc.

Published by Dodd, Mead & Company, Inc.
71 Fifth Avenue, New York, N.Y. 10003
Manufactured in the United States of America

Reissued by Dodd, Mead & Company in 1988.

Library of Congress Cataloging-in-Publication Data

Brand, Max, 1892–1944.
  Silvertip's strike.

  (The Silvertip adventure series)
  I. Title. II. Series: Brand, Max, 1892–1944.
Silvertip adventure series.
PS3511.A87S515 1988   813'.52   87–33058
ISBN 0-396-09308-6

CONTENTS

Silvertip's Strike

CHAPTER I

WYCOMBE RANCH

When Jim Silver came over the last divide, he could see the ranch house among the low foothills, and beyond the foothills was the desert. It looked like a green smudge, an olive-green drab; but he knew that at close hand the green would thin out to a sparse scattering of shrubs, all of which were arrayed in foliage which was no more than a mist, the leaves turning their edges up so as to split the full heat of the sun that would have withered them. He knew that only the toughest grass would be found yonder, and that in occasional tufts which keep a cow steadily walking as it grazes all day long.

Yet in the distance the effect of the rolling desert was green, though it was not the luminous sheen of well-watered country, but rather as grasslands appear under cloud or seen through a fog of dust. To look at that desert made the day seem overcast, though a brilliant sun was shining. The burning weight of it on the shoulders of Jim Silver told him with what force it was shining, and so did the little white streaks of salt that appeared all over the hide of his chestnut stallion where the sweat had sprung out and dried as it began to run.

The band of his sombrero was hot and soggy. He took off the hat, pulled out a bandanna, and mopped the leather band, then dried his forehead and the back of his neck. Now that his hat was off for a moment, one could see the two marks of gray hair above his temples, like small horns breaking through. He had gained his name of Silver or "Silvertip" from those spots of white hair. He was called "Arizona Jim" and other names as well, but his real name was as much a secret as the wellspring of that quiet smile which was found more often in his eyes than about his lips.

He had the look of a man who is sufficient unto himself and who relies upon greater strength than even that which appeared in his long arms and in his heavy shoulders. Or perhaps it was the stallion—a great, glimmering sheen of gold—that made him seem as much at home on the verge of the mountains and the desert as any hawk afloat in the sky.

The smile which was habitually his disappeared as he marked the gray-white of the ranch house among the hills. For he had no need to pull the letter out of his pocket; he could remember every word that Steve Wycombe had written:

DEAR SILVER: You've always hated my heart.

That's all right, because I've always hated yours, too. But now there's a chance that we can use one another. I'm asking you to come over to see me because I've got as big a job as you ever tackled in your life—and I know that you've had some big ones. Hard cash is what I'm talking about. I pay, and you take, and your job is the sort of hell fire that you prefer to breathe.

Just by accident I've heard that you're drifting north, and that's why I'm leaving this letter in Rusty Gulch in the hope that you may call for mail there.

I want you to try to forget the old days and believe that I'm talking the sort of business that you always like to hear.

Adios,

STEVE WYCOMBE

Silver recalled the words of the letter, now, as he settled the hat again on his head. And, as the shadow fell over his face, the hazel of his eyes lightened to a flicker of yellow fire, as certain types of hazel eyes can do. For he could remember very well a few of those old days when he had known Steve Wycombe before the inheriting of a ranch had removed Steve from the ranks of the professional gamblers and gunmen.

Wycombe had been half fox and half wolf. He had both teeth and cunning, plus what Jim Silver hated more than anything else in the world—the smooth and ingratiating manner of the born hypocrite.

However, the letter had called Silver across the mountains. He knew that Wycombe might be setting a trap for him, but a great part of Silver's time was spent in avoiding the traps which his enemies laid for him. Besides, there was a ring of sincerity in the words of Wycombe that led Silver to believe that the man might have fallen into a need greater than his hatred; it might be just possible that Steve was willing to forget that day when Silver had shamed him before many men in Gold Gulch.

So, for the moment, Jim Silver balanced the question nicely in his mind. At last, he rubbed the tips of his gloved fingers down the arch of the stallion's neck and murmured:

"Parade, it looks like trouble, it feels like trouble, and it probably *is* trouble. But all oats and no trouble would make us too fat to work."

He spoke again, and the stallion started down the easy slope at a trot. His rider kept no rein; but, having selected a direction, gave his mind to other things while the horse picked out the way that suited him best. He was not compelled to go over hard beds of rock if he saw going more to his taste to the right or the left; he was not forced straight on through stifling dust if he wished to take a higher route; in all things he was allowed to do pretty much as he pleased, so long as he sailed by the right star, so to speak.

If the man and the saddle had been removed and the horse considered by itself, one might have said that Parade was running wild, such was the height of his head and the free fire in his eye. There was not even a bit between his teeth, but only a light hackamore of braided horsehair. But, though he picked his own way, he remained true to the direction which had been given to him, as though from the first he had seen the low, sprawling line of the ranch house with the spider-webbing of corral fences near it.

As he went over a winding trail out of the clean brown of the sun-burned mountain slopes and into the dry mauve of the desert, Jim Silver took heed of the grazing cattle, true desert types rather roached of back and down of head; lean, active creatures which could forage actively and use their legs to go from pasture to water, even at a gallop. Off to the left, four or five miles from the house, he saw the sheen of a body of water where the spring rains had been dammed up in a "tank," and trailing out of the distance were dust clouds that rapidly approached the lake. Those were cattle on the run for moisture, and the sight of them at once told Silver the dimensions of the Wycombe ranch.

As far as the eye could reach, all of this land belonged to Steve Wycombe, and, no matter how many acres were needed to support a cow, there was enough mileage to give pasturage to a big herd. Therefore, one important fact was assured—that Wycombe had enough money to be in big trouble. For, if money is the root of all trouble, the size of the root is apt to gauge the size of the trouble.

The hands of big Jim Silver slid up inside his coat and touched the handles of the two oversize Colts which hung in spring holsters under the pits of his arms. He glanced down, also, at the Winchester which fitted into the saddle holster that sloped down under his right knee.

The ranch house was split into two wings, one section to give bunks for the hired hands, and the other for the occupancy of the owner; the kitchen was in the small link that joined the two. A windmill, whirring, moaning, clanking, arose on great skeleton legs of iron.

The possibility of digging down to water was enough to explain the presence of the house on this site. As he came closer, Silver could hear the plumping sound of the stream as it fell with a regular pulsation into the galvanized-iron tank near the mill. He thought instinctively of the days of calm when that wheel would not turn and when the long-handled pump would have to be used instead. Just inside the first corral there was a long line of troughs. If the tanks that held spring rain went dry, the cattle could be watered—in part, at least —from these troughs.

Silver went into that corral and slipped the hackamore off the head of the stallion. Parade was instantly eye-deep in the sparkle of the water. Silver watched the boluses of water glide rapidly down the throat of the horse. Again and again the dripping head of the horse was tossed up so that he could look around him, certain proof that he had known what it meant to run wild and fend for himself.

Silver put his hand on the neck of the horse, smiling, and after that Parade drank steadily, with eyes at peace, switching his tail and shrinking his hide to get off the flies that came swarming. As he finished drinking, the door of the house jerked open. A man with a pearl-gray sombrero on the back of his head, wearing a bright-yellow shirt and an unbuttoned vest, stood on the threshold for an instant; then he shouted, "Silver! Hi!" and came hurrying.

That was Steve Wycombe. Silver, watching him, knew

that he could have remembered the man by the swagger of his walk and the cant of his head. A woman appeared in the dimness of the interior of the kitchen, from the door of which Wycombe had gone out. She stood close enough to the sunshine for Silver to see that her hair was bright and that her face was young. Then she closed the door.

Perhaps she was Mrs. Steve Wycombe, poor girl!

Wycombe came up with his head to one side, nodding, smiling. He had projecting upper teeth so that he could only grin broadly with a great flash of the teeth or else hang his upper lip in a crooked sneer. The grin was very broad, just now.

There is something about buckteeth that makes a man look young and innocent. That was the appearance of Wycombe, in the main, except that his eyes could be pocketed up in wrinkles that were not always lines of mirth. He was not bad-looking, but he wore his hat like a tough, and he had his blond hair combed down over his forehead so that he had to keep tossing his head to throw back the lock out of his eyes.

"Old boy Jim Silver!" he said with emphasis.

He came up and took Silver's hand and held it through a long moment. He was one of those fellows who stand close when they speak to a man, and use their eyes up and down. That was the way he scanned Silver.

"You haven't shrunk any!" he said. "Come on in and put yourself outside a drink. I've got some seventeen-year-old rye. When I say seventeen, I don't mean seven. I'm glad to see you, you big steer!"

"I'm putting up the horse first," said Silver. "That the shed? Or do you keep all your saddle stock out?"

"That's the shed. Come along," answered Wycombe. "This is Parade, eh? He looks as though he could move. That's a shoulder! That's as fine a shoulder as I ever saw on a thoroughbred!"

6

"Watch yourself," said Jim Silver. "He'll take your arm out by the roots, if you don't."

"Savage, eh?" asked Wycombe. His step back was as swift as that of a dancer. The whole man became suddenly quick and light, and that reminded Silver of sundry unlucky fellows who had discovered the deftness of Wycombe's gun hand too late. Doctors were of very little use after Wycombe had made his play.

They put up the horse in the shed. Silver unsaddled Parade, rubbed him down with some big twists of straw, and selected the best hay he could find in the mow of the shed. There were no oats; he poured crushed barley into the feed box.

"I don't know," commented Wycombe. "Take a slick horse like that, and it's like a slick woman. Needs a lot of caring for. I don't know that it's worthwhile. Take a mustang, you throw a rope and climb on and ride as far as you want. If the bronc is used up, throw it away; it doesn't cost anything."

"Parade will stand the rough use, too," answered Silver. "But a horse is like a gun. It's better clean."

"Yeah. But when you need a gun, you need it," observed Wycombe.

"Times when I've needed Parade," said Silver, smiling.

Wycombe looked at him with a sudden seriousness, his upper lip crookedly suspended on his buckteeth.

"You've been through it, all right," he said. "You've seen everything that a man can see."

He added, rather sharply: "You used to hate my heart. What about it, Jim?"

"We can all be wrong, Wycombe," said Silver coldly.

They went back to the house in a silence, with a shadow between them; but when they reached the place, Wycombe winked and nodded.

"Want you to see something," he said, and opened the door to the kitchen.

7

The girl with the bright hair sat in a corner by the window, peeling potatoes. She had one pan in her lap, another on the floor beside her. She stood up, holding the pan between her elbows, smiling at the stranger the way Western girls are supposed to do. She had a good, straight smile, and her eyes were a stain of blue in her face. To Silver she seemed almost beautiful, which was as much as he seemed able to say about any woman.

"This is Esther Maxwell," said Wycombe. "Shake hands with her, Jim. She don't need an introduction to you. She knows about Jim Silver. Everybody knows about you. How big does he look to you, Esther?"

She kept right on smiling at Silver, as he stepped forward.

"My fingers are all sloppy from the potatoes. I can't shake hands," she said.

"How big does he look to you?" insisted Wycombe.

Silver glanced sidelong at his host.

"He looks *so* big," said the girl.

Wycombe, laughing, led the way into the next room, put his back against the door as he closed it, and winked and nodded at Silver.

"That doesn't wear the Wycombe brand, yet," he murmured, "but it's going to, boy! Pretty slick, eh? You see her dolled up for a dance and you see something. Works like a Chinaman, too."

He walked on, tapping himself on the chest, his teeth flashing.

"All for me, brother," he said.

He led the way into the next room.

"Office," he said. "All the papers and everything. Here's where little Steve works the brains; the cowboys have to work the hands."

He kept on laughing as Silver ran his glance over the square box of a room. There was one overstuffed chair in it that looked out of place, like a fur coat on a summer day.

"Sit down there while I crack open the hooch," said Wycombe. "It's going to open your eye for you, brother. But tell me first what you think of *that*."

He hooked his thumb over his shoulder.

"She's a pretty girl," said Silver.

"She's pretty *and* she's handsome. She's a performer, is what she is. All mine, brother. All for me!"

He continued to chuckle as he took a bottle out of a cupboard and filled two whisky glasses. "Just take a sock at this," he said.

Silver tasted it with his eyes studiously aslant. He smiled in honor of that noble liquor, not of his host; then they drank together.

"Now what?" asked Silver. "This is good stuff. But now what?"

Wycombe slowly thrust out his lower jaw as he answered: "Two hombres want to lift my hair. Two real bad boys. They've already started on the way. They might arrive here any old time. But when they come, they're going to find your guns working for me!"

CHAPTER II
THE FOREMAN

Wycombe held the glass in his right hand with his forefinger pointing out from it at Silver, fixing him in place, preventing speech.

"Don't talk," he said. "Wait till I get finished. Don't say 'No' till you understand why you ought to say 'Yes'! You remember me out of the old days. But I'm different now. I'm no tinhorn gambler, these days. I can play for *stakes*. And what do you think that life is worth to a rich man?"

"You're handy with a gun," said Silver. "Take care of yourself."

"I'm handy. You bet, I'm handy. But I'm bright, too. I'm so bright that I know when the other fellow has the high hand. And *two* high hands are going to be sitting in against me, before long."

"How high?" asked Silver.

"Straight flushes!" said Wycombe.

Silver sat up in his chair a little.

"I'm all right in a fight, but I'm not that right," said Wycombe. "I know it, and they know it. That makes it bad. I know they can beat me, and they know it, too. None of us are in the dark. That's what makes it bad."

"That makes it bad," said Silver.

"They're coming for me with all the cards in the world," went on Wycombe, "and they think that they've got the pot already; but I'm switching things on 'em. They're going to find me sitting against their two straight flushes with a *royal* flush. And that's you!"

He kept on jabbing his forefinger in the direction of Silver.

"If you see white water ahead, take a trip," said Silver. "For my part, I'm busy."

"Busy doing what?"

"I'm traveling."

"You are always traveling. Where?"

"Up the line," said Silver, with a vague gesture.

"No, you're not. I've got it in my pocket."

"What?"

"Your price."

"Perhaps you have," said Silver coldly.

"First, I've got you because you love a fight," said Wycombe. "I'm talking right out at you, you see? You love a fight for the fight's sake. A lot of people say that you're never in trouble till fools put you in it. But nobody ever killed your list without liking the feel of that last part of a second before the guns are going to be pulled. Answer me straight in the eyes. Do you like it? I mean, when the other fellow's eyes turn red, and he begins to show his teeth at you, and bunch his shoulders over, and his hands start working. Do you like that?"

Silver sighed and shrugged his shoulders.

"Go on with it," he said.

"Well, I'm going to hook you with the names of the hombres that are coming to lift my hair. Because, when you hear those names, your mouth is going to water. It's the sort of meat you like. It's high! The two of 'em are crooks from away back. They've both done their killings and plenty of 'em. They're stake runners. They start from scratch when it comes to guns, and one of 'em is Morris Delgas. You know Delgas?"

"I know him," said Silver.

11

"He killed Rex Walters and Lefty Markham; those are about the best two he killed. But there's others."

"I know what Morrie Delgas has done," answered Silver.

"A nice fly for a trout to rise at, eh? But the other's a shade better, even. The other's that devil of a Harry Rutherford! I don't need to ask if you know that little drink of poison! It wouldn't be healthy for you *not* to know! A little left-handed streak of misery, is what he is. Some people say he's the slickest hand with a gun that ever fanned a Colt. That's what a lot of people say. I don't know. I'd back you against him. That's all I know. And the money I put down goes into your pocket. Listen to me, Silver. When I say money, I mean it. *Big* money."

Silver shook his head and stood up slowly.

"Hey!" cried Wycombe. "Don't act that way. Wait a minute. Listen."

"I don't want to listen," said Silver.

"Wait! I'm talking something like this—five thousand apiece. I know you, Jim. You're not small time. For each one of those hombres, five thousand bucks paid on the spot."

"I don't want it," said Silver.

A moment of silence struck between them. Silver heard the ticking of a clock that was not in the room. He heard the buzzing of a big bluebottle that circled around and around the room. He smelled the aromatic sharpness of hot varnish, and knew that his body was covered with sweat, also. Wycombe was staring at him.

"Have I banked on a lame horse? Have you lost your nerve?" whispered Wycombe.

Then his voice came out with a bang. "I said five thousand. I mean it. I'll give you five thousand on account, Jim! Those hombres mean to murder me, I tell you. I'll pay you five thousand advance just to be the bodyguard!"

"I don't want the money," said Silver.

"You mean," shouted Wycombe, "that you don't want any part of my game. You don't want me!"

Silver was silent. He knew that anything could happen now, and he was ready for it, looking fixedly into the eyes of Wycombe and watching the trembling of the upper lip that hung crookedly over the buckteeth.

"I've missed!" whispered Wycombe. He cried out suddenly: "Listen to me. I can't slip up. Listen to me, Jim. I've got ten thousand dollars right here in this room. It's yours!"

Silver shook his head. A whole storm of rage and darkness poured over the eyes of Wycombe. His body trembled. His mouth kept working vainly around the prominence of those big front teeth.

"All right," he said at last, and, turning on his heel, he walked out of the room.

Silver followed him, looking left and right as he stepped cautiously through each doorway. As he went toward the back of the house, he heard the voice of Wycombe ring out ahead of him:

"What the devil do you mean by coming up here and hanging around the kitchen? Get out on the range, where you belong. Foreman? You're no foreman. You're no good. I've got a mind to fire you on the spot. I'm sick of the pretty face of you."

Silver, stepping into the kitchen, saw Wycombe in the middle of the floor, shaking his fist at a tall, brown-faced youth who stood with his sombrero in the tips of his fingers, his back to the door. On the floor he had just laid the quarters of a deer. Anger had marked the cheeks of this fellow with white, and pure rage was about to burst out of his lips when the girl intervened. She was behind the back of Wycombe, so that only Silver saw her frightened gesture of entreaty. Both hands remained for an instant pressed against her throat while her eyes talked to the foreman.

He took a great breath.

"I thought you folks might want some fresh venison, was all," said he.

He began to turn toward the door. It was very hard for him, Silver could see that, to swallow the string of insults that had just been poured at him. In a sense, Silver felt guilty, because it was plain that Wycombe felt himself enough of a gun fighter to handle this honest cow-puncher, and the wrath which he had accumulated during his interview with Silver was to be poured out now.

It was the girl who had stopped the retort that might have meant gunfire. And, if she had stopped it, most assuredly it had not been because her great concern was for Wycombe.

"I'm going to teach you," shouted Wycombe, beside himself with rage as he saw the other giving way, "I'm going to teach you that your place is out where—"

"Wait a minute, Wycombe," said Silver.

Wycombe spun about with his shoulders suddenly against the wall, the very attitude of a man who fears that he may be attacked from two sides at once.

"Hey—well, what you want?" he barked.

"I've been thinking things over," said Silver.

He felt the eyes of the girl suddenly on his face; he felt the wonder in them.

Wycombe was instantly changed. He seemed to forget his foreman in a flash.

"You mean that, Jim?" he cried. "You're going to stand by me and take a chance to—"

"I'll stand by you, I suppose," said Silver.

14

"Come on back in that room," urged Wycombe. "I'm going to pay you now to—"

"Wait a moment," said Silver.

He walked slowly toward the young foreman, who was closing the door. The latter paused, opened the door again.

"Wycombe's temper is not worth much," said Silver, "and sometimes he talks a lot."

He held out his hand with a smile.

"My name is Jim Silver," he said.

The white face of the foreman turned crimson. He knew, it was clear, that this gesture on the part of Silver was purely in token that the stranger had overheard but had not lost respect for the foreman because he had taken water in the row. Never was a stronger grasp laid on the hand of Silver.

"I'm Dan Farrel," said he. "And—thanks. It's great to meet you, Silver. It's great!"

He went out, closing the door hastily behind him, as though he wished to conceal something that was coming into his face.

Silver, turning, saw Wycombe beckoning impatiently at the other door of the kitchen. He saw, also, one flash of gratitude and astonishment in the eyes of the girl. Then he went on through the door with Wycombe and back into the study.

"You gave me a turn, Silver." Steve Wycombe laughed. "You can throw a bluff with anybody I ever saw. I thought for a minute that you meant what you said. Wait a minute. Ten thousand, I said, and ten thousand it's going to be."

He started to unlock the door of a big square-faced safe that filled a corner of the room.

"No," said Silver. "I don't want the cash."

"You don't want what?" shouted Wycombe.

"I don't take blood money," said Silver.

Wycombe straightened his body with jerks and finally faced his guest with a frown.

"I never was able to figure you out," he said. "You beat me—but that's all right. As long as you're with me, anything's all right! Only—"

He paused, and then shrugged his lean shoulders twice.

"About that fellow Farrel," he said. "Why did you make that funny play about him? Going up and shaking hands with the bum when he'd just backed down and taken water like a cur?"

"He's not a cur. He's a man," said Silver. "And I'd rather murder a man than shame him."

CHAPTER III

SILVER LISTENS

They sat for a time in the office. Wycombe drank more of the old rye whisky. Silver smoked cigarettes and did the listening, as a rule.

He had merely said: "Let's find out why the pair are after you. It's quite a time since you were in the games where you rubbed elbows with the pair of 'em. Two or three years, I should say."

"All that matters," said Wycombe, "is that they're after me, and that you know what they look like."

"No," said Silver. "I need to know more."

Wycombe curled his upper lip to speak, and once more the lip stayed curled on the projecting teeth while Wycombe changed his mind about the words he was to have spoken.

"Well," he said at last, "you won't be a hired man. You're going to have your full share in the show."

He struck out his jaw after the way he had, and tossed back the blond hair.

"I'm sorry I got sore in front of the girl," he said suddenly. "You think she noticed?"

"She noticed," said Silver.

"What did she look like?" asked Wycombe.

"Frightened," said Silver.

Wycombe lolled back in his chair, suddenly at ease.

"It don't do any harm to throw a scare into a jane,"

17

he declared. "Let 'em know that there's a real man around, and they like it all the better. You know what I mean."

"I know what you mean," said Silver, probing the dark and mean soul of the man with a steady eye.

But Wycombe failed to understand the glance. He went on: "You know how it is. A girl likes to see a man that's up to something. She doesn't want to have a yellow pup around. She's always liked that foreman of mine pretty well. She'll hate his heart from now on. Eh?"

"Perhaps," said Silver.

"They know my record, around here," went on Wycombe. "They know that I'm no soft-handed baby. Eh?"

"They ought to know that."

"But, going back a little—I'm kind of beat by you, Silver. You throw ten thousand dollars out the window?"

Silver shrugged his shoulders.

"I want to be my own man," said he. "I want to do as I please. And I don't want blood money. I never took any, and I don't want it."

"But you'll hire out—you'll stay here, I mean—and keep àn eye out for me?"

"I'll stay here—for a while. If Morrie Delgas and Harry Rutherford show up, I'll try my hand fighting for you. I'll work for you as though you'd paid me the money, Wycombe—unless you start kicking things around."

"Kicking you around?" said Wycombe, laughing. "I'm not a half-wit, old son."

"Let's hear the story of why the pair are on your trail."

"Why pick on that? Why does it matter?"

"Because," said Silver, "the cause that puts a man on a trail is the grindstone that sharpens the edge of him. I want to know what sort of a temper and edge these fellows are wearing."

Wycombe considered gloomily. He made himself a cigarette and then remarked:

"You know Gold Gulch?"

"Yes."

"Know Fourth Street?"

"Yes."

"Know the pawnshop on the corner?"

"Pudge Wayland used to run it."

"That's right. Know anything more about Pudge?"

"He was a crook and a fence."

"He was a crook and a fence, all right," said Wycombe. "Know what happened to him?"

"He was shot."

"By whom?" asked Wycombe.

"I never heard."

"Nobody else did, except a few. I'm the fellow that killed him."

Silver actually sighed with relief.

"Is that what's behind this trail that Morrie Delgas and Rutherford are on?"

"That's it!" said Steve Wycombe, brightening. "I ought to have a medal and a vote of thanks for getting that fat Gila monster out of the world, instead of inheriting trouble about it, eh?"

"It seems that way. How did the thing happen?"

"I'd had words with him. It was a couple of years back. I'd had words with him. About nothing much. Just about a loan he'd made me on a gold watch. I was sore. The next time I saw him, I was coming out of the mouth of an alley. It was night. I saw the fat back of Pudge Wayland come across the street. I sang out and swore at him. He whirled around. I was drunk. I was on a mean drunk. You know, the kind when you don't know what you're doing. I thought I saw a gun in his hand. I shot him dead. That's all."

He stuck out his lower jaw and stared at the floor.

"That's all—except that he wasn't even wearing a gun?" suggested Silver.

"The fool," said Steve Wycombe, "should 'a' had one

19

on, anyway. There was a witness, y'understand? A sap of a no-good sneak thief. He saw everything. He spotted me. I had to give him a regular pension to keep his mouth shut. And he went off into Mexico, where he'd be safe in case I decided to pay him the rest of his pension with a chunk of lead. He stayed down there and collected my checks. Just like that. And then the blockhead goes and gets into a row, a while ago, and gets himself knifed up, and the doctors say that he's going to die, and he lies there on the floor of a saloon and tells what he knows to the fellow that knifed him. Makes a confession, d'you see? And the fellow that knifed him is Harry Rutherford, and with Harry is that Morrie Delgas.

"Well, this is how the thing all hitches together. That Pudge Wayland was a fence, and you know it. And he'd done a lot of work for Delgas and for Rutherford, both of 'em, because they were working hand in glove. And when Wayland died, he had a whole slew of stolen goods on his hands, and a big pile of it belonged to those two thugs.

"You see what had happened? I bump off Pudge Wayland. His heirs get everything in his shop—and it's a ton! They clean out his safe. They get themselves rich, and gyp Morrie and Harry out of a whole little fortune in honest stolen goods they'd given to Pudge. That must have been the way of it.

"Anyway, my man lies there on the floor of the cantina and talks his fool head off, and he sees that pair shake hands over him and swear that they'll go and bump off Wycombe, just to even the account. They'd always hated me, anyway, since a little poker game we once played together. And then the fool fellow, he doesn't die, after all; but he gets better, and he's honest enough to write me a letter and tell me how he happened to put

20

those two bloodhounds on my trail. But you see the funny part?"

"I don't know what part would be funny to you," said Silver.

"Why," said Wycombe, "ain't it a scream that'd curdle your blood to think of me bumping off a fat fool like Pudge Wayland and then getting a pair of wildcats like those two dropped right down my back?"

CHAPTER IV
SILVER GIVES WARNING

The evening came on, and Jim Silver was glad of a chance to get out of the tobacco reek and whisky smell of the closed house into the open. Besides, there was something unusual—rain promised over the desert, and thunder bumping and rumbling in the sky just like carts going over iron bridges.

Steve Wycombe went off by himself for a few moments, and Silver was gladdest of all to be alone. He wanted to do some thinking. He had come to the hardest moment of all, which is when a man tries to untangle his own actions and discover the motives of them. He kept telling himself that he was a fool to have bound himself to fight for this fellow Wycombe and, above all, to have bound himself against such formidable men as Morris Delgas and that ravenous ghost of a man, Harry Rutherford.

Certainly it was not compassion for Wycombe that kept him on the place. He could hardly put his finger on the cause until he saw young Dan Farrel walk from the first corral toward the bunk house. Then he could remember and be sure that it was something about Farrel and the girl that had turned the scales and induced him to stay. Why?

Well, he could not say exactly. He was simply a prospector in the land of trouble, and there seemed to be a rich strike of danger and complications straight ahead of him.

A pair of cow-punchers came away from the horse shed and ran sneaking up on their foreman. They were almost on him when he sidestepped. There was a swift flurry of action, an uproar of laughing voices, and the foreman went on, leaving his two men to pick themselves up from the ground. Jim Silver was pleased enough to smile. He waved Farrel over to him.

"What do you say about rain, Farrel?" he asked.

Farrel shook his head. "It's the wrong season," he declared. "You don't know how rain comes here—just a few drops at a time—just enough to keep the lips wet and the patient from dying. Just enough water to keep the grass from dying clear down to the bottom of its roots. This is a dry ranch, Silver!"

He nodded and smiled as he spoke.

"You like it." said Jim Silver. "There's something about it you like, or that you expect to like later on."

"Why do you say that?"

"Because you'll put up with a good deal in order to stay on it. Why, Farrel? There are plenty of jobs everywhere for good cowmen."

Farrel stared at him. Then turning toward the foot-hills, he waved his hand west and north and east.

"You see how those mountains are heaped up in three bunches? Over there to the east are the Kendals—that's old Mount Kendal back there in blue and white, just on the right. Over here, straight north, that second bunch make up the Humphreys Mountains. I don't have to tell you which is Mount Humphreys itself. Look at the way it goes jump into the sky! Now, yonder on the left, right over there bang against the west, you see the biggest of the three bunches? Those are the Farrel Mountains."

Silver looked not so much at the silhouette of ragged blackness in the west, not so much at the three vast

23

masses of cumulus clouds which were blossoming over the three groups of mountains, as he did into the lean, brown face of Dan Farrel. For it seemed to Silver that some of the fire and grandeur of the sunset mountains was reflected in the face of the cow-puncher.

"I see," said Silver. "They were named after one of your tribe?"

"Great-grandfather. Ever since his day there's always been a Farrel on this ground."

He hooked his thumb over his shoulder.

"It isn't the house that matters. I don't give a hang about that. It's the ground that counts. I've gone away and worked on other places—places on the ledge of the desert, like this, with mountains close by that were a lot bigger and finer than those three outfits—but I never found a place that fitted into my head the way this one does. Every time I lay an eye on those mountains, it's as though I'd daubed a rope on a maverick and added it to my herd. I tell you what, Silver—it may seem a funny thing to you, but it's true—it seems to me that I know every wave of the ground off there to the south from the ranch house. I know just where the waves of the land are running, every one of 'em."

"How did the Farrels lose the place?" asked Silver.

"My old man gambled it away to Wycombe's old man, that's the whole story."

"You hate to leave it?"

"The way you'd hate to stop breathing."

"Well," said Silver, "it looks as though you'd have to go."

"Does it?"

"On account of the girl."

"What d'you mean?"

"I've been talking to Wycombe, and he wants her. If he thinks you're in his way, with her, he'll cut your throat. He'll fire you off the ranch, at least."

24

"What makes you think that there's anything between the girl and me?" asked Dan Farrel.

"I saw her turning white and pink, to-day in the kitchen. Farrel, you'll have to move."

Farrel took off his hat, mopped his forehead, and then stood with the hat crushed in his two hands. Slowly his glance went across the mountains from the east to the west, until he was facing the last fire of the sunset. He said nothing, but, after a moment, he walked away and left Silvertip in profoundly gloomy thought. Tragedy was not ten steps away from the Wycombe ranch, he felt, and it was probably even nearer than those expert gunmen, Morrie Delgas and Harry Rutherford; in fact, it probably was stepping in the boots of Dan Farrel.

Nothing like this had ever come into the ken of Jim Silver.

Through the open kitchen window, he saw the girl moving back and forth rapidly, with the haste of a cook who is making the last preparations for the service of a meal. He went to the window and leaned an elbow on the sill. The girl was pouring the water off a pot of boiled potatoes; a cloud of steam rushed up from the sink about her shoulders and head. Then she spilled the potatoes into a great dish.

"Suppose," said Silver, without an introductory word, "that a fellow had a good pair of hands, plenty of work anywhere he wanted to find it, and a girl willing to travel anywhere in the world with him; couldn't he be happy off the home ground?"

She had turned half toward him, though without looking into his face. It was as if his words had arrested her whole mind so that a greater and a greater tension was put on her. He saw it in the stiffening of her body, in the way her head lifted. Afterward, she came to the window to confront him closely.

"How much has Danny told you?" she asked.

25

"Not as much as I told him," answered Jim Silver. "Do you know how close you are to trouble?"

"From Steve Wycombe?" she asked.

"He's going to ask you to marry him. How long can you put him off? He's used to having his own way."

She took a deep, quick breath. The shake of her head was a shudder through her entire body.

"I don't know," she answered. "I can't get Danny to leave the place."

"You'll have to," responded Silver. "You'll have to persuade him fast, too. Wycombe wants you. He wants you as much as he can want anything. If you put him off, he'll be suspicious. If he grows suspicious, he can't help finding out that there's something between you and Farrel. And if he guesses that—" He paused.

"I know," said the girl. "He'd murder Dan in a moment, I suppose. I'm going to leave! I'll leave tonight. I'll leave now!"

"You'd better," said Silver. He pitied her, suddenly, more than he had ever pitied any other human being. The trouble which faced her seemed so totally unfair. "There's only one other thing to do—and that's to persuade Danny to live in another place."

"It's no good. He has desert fever, and the only desert he can live in is this one. He's tried to go away before this. But he came back looking like a ghost. It's the sort of homesickness that doesn't fade out."

"Have you got a horse of your own?" Silver asked her.

"I have."

"Have you money?"

"No. Only a little."

"I can help you out with some cash."

"If I have to step out of his life—out of Danny's life —forever—" she murmured.

Then she straightened herself and smiled wanly at Silver.

"I can't even say good-by to him, I suppose," she said.

"No, I suppose not," said Silver.

He reached for his wallet and opened it.

"Take this," said he, and offered a sheaf of bills. But she only shook her head.

"I can't do it," she told him. "I can manage with what I have."

Silver put the money back into the wallet, stared at her, and then walked away into the dusk. His thoughts were so baffled, so gloomy, that he kicked aimlessly at the ground over which he walked. He had been in tangles before, but none so thoroughly complicated as this one. The chief anger he felt was directed toward Farrel. The fellow looked as hard as nails, but his weakness was what is the strength of other men—an overmastering love for one place.

Into the darkening north Silver looked, toward the mountains. They were new enough to him, and yet already they began to stand in his mind like old, familiar faces. He remembered how Farrel had pointed to them; he remembered the reverence and affection with which the voice of Farrel had uttered the names. After all, a man cannot be blamed for passions which are bigger than himself.

He went to the pump and sloshed a tin pan full of cold water. There was soap, yellow and strong, to wash with, and a big, coarse scrubbing brush. He worked on his finger tips until he had got the leather grease out from under the nails. The rest of his washing took very little time. He managed to find a clean spot on one of the big roller towels and dried himself.

The cow-punchers were all around him, sputtering in the water, swearing as the soap got into recent cuts. One of them was red-headed, the clown of the lot. He squared off in front of Silver, swaying thick shoulders.

"He ain't so big," said "Red." "I'll take you on for a couple of rounds, big boy." ⸰

He began to dance on the tips of his toes, easing his hands back and forth in readiness to strike or to parry. Silver finished drying his own hands and smiled.

"Come on!" said Red, as the others began to crow and whoop. "Come on!" said Red. "Nobody gets by on reputation in this man's ranch. Let's see what you've got, Jim Silver!"

He was dancing, still swaying himself from side to side a little, when Silver made a flashing gesture with both arms and caught the two hands of Red. He kept on smiling as he crushed those hands until he could feel the supple bones springing and giving.

"In my part of the world, we shake before we fight," said Silver.

He released the hands and stepped back. Red began to open and close his fingers, laughing.

"In my part of the world, when a gent shakes hands like that, we don't fight him," said Red.

The other punchers were laughing, too. The supper gong rang. Silver went in with the rest, and by the brightness of their eyes he knew that he would have no more signs of trouble from them. They had accepted him as something more than a large bubble of reputation.

CHAPTER V
GUNS IN THE DARK

As the punchers entered, their employer was revealed walking up and down at the head of the dining room. He had dressed for dinner by buttoning his vest, sleeking the blond forelock with water, and slipping a pair of brilliant elastic garters over his sleeves to leave his wrists supple and free. As the spurs jingled and the heels thundered on the wooden floor, Mr. Wycombe made a movement of his hand that stopped every one. Then he said:

"You waddies have gotta know that there are two thugs steering for this ranch, right now, and aiming to collect my scalp when they arrive. If they look in through the window and start blazing away while we're having supper, they might smash up a lot of crockery. So one of you stand guard outside. Red, you take a turn. Ten or fifteen minutes and you can come back inside and somebody else will take the beat. The hombres I talk about are Morrie Delgas and that skinny little streak of murder, Harry Rutherford. If they start raising the devil, maybe my friend, Jim Silver, will help my song and dance. That's all, boys. Set down and feed your faces."

Red took a handful of biscuits, wedged some butter into them, and left the room to stand guard. The other punchers sat down. The chairs rumbled like thunder. Dishes and cutlery began to clatter. Some one asked

29

Wycombe what Delgas and Rutherford had against him.

"Just old chums gone wrong," said Wycombe.

There were heaps of food—venison steaks, two great bowls of baked beans with a rich scum browned over the tops of them, heaps of biscuits with snowy flanks and crusty tops, mountains of potatoes, huge dishes of gravy. Forks and spoons dug into these treasures. Presently heads were seriously bent; the girl came in and filled the ponderous drinking cups from a pail of coffee. She wore a faint, fixed smile. She reminded Silver of a prize fighter sick with punishment but smiling to show that everything is all right.

When she came by Wycombe, he lifted his head and smiled like a calf at her. Then he resumed his former position, his brow reclining in the palm of his left hand while with the right he casually and in the most disinterested fashion scooped food toward his face. A profound loathing began to work at the very roots of the soul of Jim Silver.

The better the food, the swifter the eating on a Western ranch. Those punchers walked through the provisions on the table and then rolled cigarettes and sipped a second beaker of coffee. They said things to Esther as she went the round, pouring it out. "Regular good stuff," said one, and another: "Where you cook, this cowboy camps." Some of them said: "How's things?" Every one muttered something; up to that time no one had seemed aware of her existence, except Wycombe.

The second round of coffee was finished. Whirls, clouds, long streaks of cigarette smoke hung in the air as the punchers rose, one after another, and went out. Their footfalls boomed through the room, then grew dim and muffled in the dust outside. The smoke seemed to be collecting around the two lamps that stood on the table. There remained at the table only the foreman, Silver, and Wycombe, as the girl came in to clear the dishes away. When she went past Wycombe, he put out his arm and gathered her suddenly into the hollow of it.

"How's things?" asked Wycombe, smiling up at her.

She only smiled down at him vaguely. Danny Farrel grew rigid in his chair.

"I've got to finish my work," said Esther Maxwell. "Please, Steve."

"Maybe you're going to stop working, pretty soon," said Wycombe. "Maybe there's going to be a Chinaman or something for you to boss. Maybe—"

"Esther!" barked Farrel.

Wycombe released her suddenly. She stepped back.

"Eight o'clock and all's well," drawled the puncher who walked on guard outside the windows.

Farrel and Wycombe were staring at one another, Farrel still rigid, and Wycombe leaning loosely forward. In the middle of a smile, his upper lip had caught again over his projecting teeth and stayed there in a snarl. The girl hurried out of the room with a pile of empty dishes. Silver folded his arms, because in that position his hands were close to his guns. It seemed strange to him that the girl should have left the room, unaware that there was murder in the air. He himself could hear the bumping of blood against his temples as his heart beat faster and stronger.

"You've got the say with her, have you?" said Wycombe.

Farrel was as straight as a stick and pale as a stone; he had his two hands on the edge of the table. The hands of Wycombe were out of sight.

"I hate to see a girl mauled around," said Farrel.

"You hate to see it, do you?" answered Wycombe.

He worked his lips until they closed; he moistened them with the swift red tip of his tongue.

Farrel pushed back his chair.

31

"I'll be going on," he murmured slowly.

He stood up.

"Wait a minute," commanded Wycombe. "I'm going to find out something."

Farrel halted, halfway to the door.

Wycombe had pushed back his chair and sat forward on the edge of it with his hands still out of sight.

"I wanta know," said Steve Wycombe, "what that girl is to you, Farrel."

"Never mind. Nothing!" said Farrel.

"I'm not to never mind, eh?" said Wycombe. He laughed suddenly, turning all white around the mouth and with a devil in his eyes. "Why, Farrel, who *are* you?"

Farrel said nothing.

Wycombe gasped: "You're going to tell me what to do and how to act in my own house, are you? You're going to tell me how to treat a girl, are you? You dirty rat, what's the girl to you?"

"I'm going to marry her, that's all," said Farrel.

The door opened. The girl came back, not in time to hear anything, but in time to see the attitudes of the two men. She cried out in fear.

"Listen to me—you, Esther," said Wycombe. "Have you been fooling me? Have you been making a fool of me? This bum of a secondhand foreman says that he's going to marry you. Is that straight?"

"Oh, Danny!" mourned the girl.

The way she put out her hands toward Farrel told Steve Wycombe enough.

"You sneaking thief!" he yelled, and came out of his chair with a gun in each hand. "I'm going to—"

"Back up!" called Silver, and shot the left-hand gun out of the grasp of Wycombe.

"You? You, too?" screamed Wycombe. I'll get you both. I'll—I'll—"

He dived under the table and heaved up the side of it with a lift of his shoulders. The whole mass of crockery went to the floor. The lamps were dashed out. Darkness blotted the room, and the scream of the girl made a red zigzag like lightning across the brain of Silver.

It was not complete darkness. The flame of one lamp had ignited the oil that spread out from it in a thin layer on the floor. A blue welter of fire began to play, keeping the room awash with uncertain ebbing and flowing of shadows. Outside, the guard was shouting; the girl had not stopped screaming.

Silver, flat on his stomach in a corner of the room, extended two guns before him and waited. A gun spat fire twice from close to the opposite wall. The voice of Farrel, near the windows, cursed briefly.

"I've got one of you!" screamed Wycombe.

There was the loose impact of a falling body against the floor. The guard was shouting, near the door:

"What the devil's up? What's happening?"

He was afraid to come in, of course.

The gun of Wycombe flashed again, and Silver shot at the glint of the face that he saw behind the little red tongue of fire. He almost felt the impact of his bullet tearing through flesh and bone.

A voice said, "Ah!"

That was Wycombe. There was no vocal strength to the sound; he simply breathed the word out. "Light!" said Wycombe. And now his voice had a great weakness of shuddering in it. "Light! I'm dying! I'm sick—"

The screaming of the girl was ended. That was one good thing. Farrel said nothing. Perhaps he was dead.

Silver went across the room to where Wycombe lay. The burning oil gave only the dimmest sort of a light, but it was enough for him to see that Farrel had been kneeling against the wall between the two windows; the

33

body of the girl lay flat near the kitchen door; and Wycombe had slipped down with his head pressing at a breaking angle against the wall.

"Get a lantern, Farrel," said Silver.

"Esther's dead!" shouted Farrel. "Help! He's murdered her."

Other voices, many footfalls were heard outside the door. Someone carried a lantern, its light swinging wildly across the windows and intercrossing swift shuttles of brightness over the ceiling.

The lantern was brought into the room, and showed Farrel holding the limp body of the girl in his arms. Her head hung down; her arms and legs trailed toward the floor. The wave of cow-punchers advanced in a solid mass.

"Wycombe, did you shoot at the girl?" murmured Silver.

"No!" said Wycombe. "I wish I had. I'm dying. You got me, you sneak, you traitor! I wish I'd killed you all!"

The lantern light came close and flooded over him. His whole breast was flowing with blood, it seemed. The blood ran down to the floor and gathered in two pools. The body of Wycombe was still. His arms lay limply at his sides, with the hands turned palm up. But his face was working violently, the lips covering and uncovering the gleam of the teeth.

"Take Silver!" he said. "Red, Joe, Lefty, Mack, take Silver. He murdered me. He killed me right here. The skunk—he killed me! Shoot him to pieces!"

They looked at one another; they looked at Silver; they looked vaguely back at their employer.

One of the lot helped Farrel with the girl. She had only fainted, it appeared, and now she began to moan. They carried her out of the shambles.

Silver said: "Wycombe found out that Farrel is going to marry Esther. He went crazy and pulled his guns on

34

Farrel. I knocked one gun out of his grip. He threw the table over and tried to shoot up the lot of us. That was why I plugged him. A dirty business, but it had to be done."

He kneeled beside Wycombe in an effort to feel his pulse.

"Don't touch me. Keep your murdering hands away from me," said Wycombe, in a horrible, bubbling voice. "Boys, don't believe him. He's lying. Tear him apart. Let me see you split him open. I've got a thousand dollars for the man who—"

"Shut up, Steve," said a voice from the doorway. "He only stole a march on us."

Silver saw two men at the entrance of the room, one a great, hairy brute, and the other small and dapper, with a pale face. He knew that Delgas and Rutherford had arrived too late.

CHAPTER VI
WYCOMBE'S WILL

Some of the men threw sand on the burning oil and put it out. At the directions of Silver, two more dragged in a mattress, with the blankets folded to lift his head and shoulders, for when he lay flat his own blood choked him.

Silver cut away the clothes, tried to stop the bleeding in chest and back with handfuls of dust, and bound a thick bandage made of a torn sheet around and around the scrawny body. Hollow-chested, lean of shoulders and arms, Wycombe looked no more than a boy. It had only been his spirit that made him dangerous, and the same spirit was still green in his eyes. He kept rolling his glance from Delgas to Silver to Rutherford.

"Give me a shot of hooch," he said. "I've got some thinking to do."

Silver tilted his head and applied a bottle of whisky to the lips. Wycombe drank it like water. Afterward he closed his eyes for a long moment, but he was not dead. Silver could see the pulse beat in the scrawny hollow of the throat.

"I wanta have a pen and paper," said Wycombe. "Silver, you write down what I say. I'm going to make my will."

One of the men ran off to get what was needed.

Rutherford sat down on the floor beside Wycombe.

"I'm sorry to see you this way, Steve," said he. "I hoped that you'd be up and about when we arrived. You're not much use to us this way, Steve. We've been killing you every day for a long time. Now that you're passing out on your own hook, there doesn't seem to be anything left for us to do. The world's a hollow place for us, with you out of it!"

"Yeah?" murmured Wycombe. "He shot me in the dark. He sided with that rat of a Farrel of mine. And I'd hired Silver to keep the two of you away from me."

"Had you?" said Rutherford.

He turned his thin, handsome face toward Jim Silver and smiled.

"Old Jim Silver," he said softly. "Always up to something."

Delgas came and put his hands on his knees. The hair grew like fur down to the second knuckles.

"How d'you feel, kid?" he asked.

"There's hands inside of me tearing me apart," said Wycombe.

"Too bad," said Delgas, and began to grin widely, nodding at Wycombe. "We had lots of hell, but it's better than nothing to get a flash of you when you're like that."

"You swine!" breathed Steve Wycombe.

"Let him alone, Delgas," said Silver. "Get up and stand back from him, Rutherford. He's a dying man."

"Oh," said Rutherford. "You don't like my manners, Silver?"

He rose slowly, still smiling.

"I don't like your manners," said Silver.

He looked at them calmly.

"Now!" whispered Wycombe, his eyes burning. "Are you going to take water from him, the pair of you? Jump him—blow him to pieces, boys! I'll thank you, and I'll pay you for doing it! It'll make a red-letter day in your lives, the cash I'll give you!"

"And be mobbed by this gang when we open up? We're not such fools," said Rutherford.

He stepped back. Wycombe glowered at Silver.

"I've got no luck," he said.

"You'll be hearing from us, Silver," said Delgas.

"Thanks," said Silver. "Come and take tea with me, one day. Any old time would suit me."

The paper and ink and pen arrived. Silver sat down cross-legged and dipped the pen and poised it above the writing pad.

"Go ahead, Wycombe," he suggested.

"I want this to sound like law," said Wycombe. "Write like this. Put the date down and the place, first. Then say: 'I, Stephen Wycombe, being in my right mind and the full possession of my faculties, make this my last will and testament.' How does that sound to you, boys? Legal?"

The cow-punchers formed an outer semicircle. Some of them were standing. Some were sitting on their heels, watching.

"It sounds like a book," said one of them.

"That's the way you gotta sound, or else the lawyers will take you all apart," said Wycombe. "Somebody wipe my mouth. I don't seem to have any hands."

Red came close and wiped the bloody lips with a bandanna. He gave Wycombe another taste of the whisky.

"It's hard," said Wycombe, "to think of losing out on all of that seventeen-year-old rye! Go on writing, Silver. 'Last will and testament. It takes the place of, and makes null, all other wills and testaments that I may have made.' You see, I haven't made any other wills; but you've got to talk like that in a will."

He went on: "I give, devise, and bequeath to my dear friend, Morris Delgas, one third of all the bulls, steers, cows, and calves in my possession."

"Hey," said Delgas. "What's this?"

38

"Shut up!" whispered Wycombe. "I gotta keep enough breath to finish. Go on writing, Silver. 'One half of all my land, except as shall hereinafter be excepted.' How's that for fancy talk? I was educated all right. A lot of good my education has done me! Go on: 'And to my dear friend, Henry Rutherford, I give, devise, and bequeath one third of all the live stock in my possession, together with one half of my land, except as shall be hereinafter excepted.' Have you got that?"

"I have it," said Silver, working with a rapid pen.

"Well," murmured Harry Rutherford softly, "this is the richest thing that I ever heard of. Where does the poison come in, Wycombe?"

"Wait a minute. He's having his joke," said Delgas. "The catch is going to come now."

"Go on writing," urged Wycombe. "And to my dear friend called variously Arizona Jim, Silvertip, Silver, Jim Silver, and other aliases—I mean the man who caught the famous wild horse, Parade—I give, devise, and bequeath all the cash in my possession, together with the debts which I owe and one third of all the live stock on my place. In addition I give, devise, and bequeath to Jim Silver, alias Arizona Jim, alias Silvertip, all the water rights to the big tank called Johnson's Lake, and I give him outright the house and the corrals and all the ground in every direction for one half mile from the ranch house.' There, boys, that looks like a pretty even split, to me. Silver don't get any land to speak of, but he gets cash and water. Give me that to sign, Jim, will you?"

Silver held the pad before him. Wycombe, with a twitching mouth, scratched on his signature.

"That look all right and legal, Silver?" asked Wycombe.

"It looks right enough to me," said Silver.

"Sign it, then. Everybody in the room sign it. Silver, write down: 'Witnessed this day by me,' and then the rest of you sign under that place. Understand?"

The paper was accordingly passed around. Wycombe lay back, nodding a little as he heard the scratching of the pen. Once Silver found the eyes of the dying man fixed upon him with a deathless malice and hatred.

"The gent that should have guarded me, he shoots me down!" said Wycombe. Then, suddenly, he asked: "Where's the girl and where's Farrel? Go call 'em in, will you? I wanta say good-by to them. I gotta remember my manners and say good-by to all of my old friends."

He closed his eyes. His mouth opened. Silver could no longer see the beat of the pulse in the hollow of the throat. When he touched the face of Wycombe, he found the skin clammy with cold sweat.

One of the punchers came back, bringing the girl and tall Dan Farrel. She held back. Farrel had an arm about her, supporting her forward. Her eyes were doubly large in the pallor of her face.

So the two of them came before the dying man.

"They're here," said Silver.

The eyes of Wycombe fluttered and then opened. He frowned to bring his attention on the pair.

"Farrel and Esther. Fine-looking pair, eh?" he muttered. "The two of you—I want to say something to you. You're the ones that knifed me. Except because of your pretty mug, Esther, I'd be all right now. I'd be drinking rye and taking it easy, instead of going where I'm bound. I—" He gasped.

"Whisky!" he whispered.

Silver poured a large dram down his throat. He coughed and strangled feebly over it. The bubbling of his voice became greater, as though some of the liquid were in his lungs.

He said: "I never wasted time on girls before I saw you, Esther."

"Steve," cried the girl, "I never wanted to lead you on. I never said a word to you. The only reason that I didn't tell you right away that I loved Danny was because I was afraid that he'd be fired, and he can't live away from this place."

"Yeah? Can't he?" murmured Wycombe. "He'll damned well live away from it, now that these three hombres have the place. And this is what I wanta say to the pair of you: I hope you have nothing but rotten bad luck. I hope the pair of you get sickness and meanness. I hope you start in hating each other. If you have kids, I hope that they're halfwits and that they're sick every day of their lives. I hope you're broke and stay broke. I hope you have to beg, and folks kick you out of their way. If there's anything in the curse of a dying man, I put it on—"

His head dropped back. The girl, with her hands pressed before her eyes, shut out the grisly picture of the dying man.

"Take me away, Danny!" she murmured.

"I put—a curse," muttered Wycombe, "on—on—"

He bit at the air, writhed his legs together, and sat bolt upright.

"I can't breathe!" he gasped. "Give me air—whisky. I—"

Blood bubbles broke on his lips. He twisted suddenly, fell on his side, and lay still.

Silver leaned close above him for an instant, then turned him on his back and closed the eyes. Wycombe was smiling in death as in life, with his upper lip caught crookedly across his projecting teeth. Silver, with a fold of the blanket, covered that repulsive face.

He stood up and faced the silence of the group.

"Friends," he said, "the law is going to put an eye on all of this. You fellows jot down everything that you can remember of exactly what's happened. You'll have to answer questions. One thing is straight—I killed Wycombe. I shot him to keep him from murdering

41

Farrel—and myself. Farrel, were you hurt?"

"A graze along the ribs," said Dan Farrel. "It's nothing."

"Lemme tell you all something," boomed the great bass voice of Morris Delgas. "I dunno just how it's going to work out, but this here Wycombe was always a poison rat. It looks like he's done something for us, but before we get through we'll find out that he's put a knife through us, every one. I'm going to go out and get some fresh air."

CHAPTER VII

THE NEW MANAGER

A coroner came out from Pepper Gulch the next morning and made an examination. He was an old-timer with a dull-blue eye and tobacco-stained blond mustache. His examination lasted not more than half an hour, after which he pronounced over a glass of rye whisky, aged seventeen years:

"The way it looks to me, it would be pretty hard to kill a gent like Steve Wycombe without doin' it in self-defense. I dunno that you could pick up any jury around this part of the world that would accuse a man of nothin' more than self-defense even if there was eye-witnesses that seen somebody bash Steve over the head when his back was turned."

The reputation of Wycombe was in this manner its own reward. The body was carted to the town to be buried in the plot where other and hardly more honorable ancestors had lain before him, and the will which he had signed was promptly recorded and filed.

The result was that the three to whom the inheritance had so strangely come could enter upon the possession at once. It was not many days later that they held a conference in the very room that had formerly been the office of the dead man.

Morris Delgas, because he was the oldest and the largest of the trio, presided. He sat not in a chair but on the

43

desk, with his shirt open and his sleeves rolled up. The man was everywhere furred over with black hair. His forehead was wide and very low, with a knob at either corner of it to match the cheek bones beneath. He looked like a perfect specimen for the prize ring, now grown a little overweight.

He wore new boots, graced with golden, spoon-handled spurs; but otherwise he showed no token of the sudden good fortune that had come to him, for his clothes were those which any cow-puncher might have donned as a working outfit. His shirt was blue flannel, in spite of the heat of the weather; his hat was a very battered old felt, and the only evidence of wealth lay in the golden spurs and in the great fat cigar into which he had sunk his teeth.

He liked the feel of it so well that he could not relax the grip of his teeth for an instant. The oily stain ran across his mouth. The tongue with which he licked those lips became stained, also. But he never touched the cigar with his hand. He smoked it rarely in puffs, but let it burn slowly with the movements of his breath, and when he changed its position, it was done by manipulations of the teeth and the tongue. In fact, he was a formidable brute of a man. His body looked too gross for activity, but his eye was as bright as the eye of a wild cat.

Sitting there on the desk, with his huge back turned to the windows, he literally cast a shadow over the other two men.

"Gents," he said, "we gotta get together. We gotta find out what was in the crazy bean of Steve Wycombe when he passed us this ground, and then we gotta see how we can pull together. Because look at the lay of the land. Me and Harry have got half the acres. And, believe me, there's some acres! I been out and rode all around the place, and it's a long day's ride. And we each got a third of the live stock, along with you, Silver. But there's an-

44

other way of lookin' at the thing. We got the land and
our shares of the stock. But you got the most part of
the water, if not all. Except for some shallow kind of
pools that stand a while around in the spring rains, there
ain't no water on the rest of the place. The cows have
gotta come in to the big tank or else they've gotta come
right in here to the home place. It's a funny business,
and I guess that the brains must have run with the blood
right out of poor old Steve! Now's the time for us to
talk a spell and keep shut up afterward."

"Wycombe wasn't crazy," said Harry Rutherford. "Not
a bit."

"What was he, then?" asked big Delgas.

"He was out for blood, that's all," said Rutherford.

"Go on, handsome, and tell me what you mean," said
Delgas.

"Aw, you tell him, Silver," said Rutherford. "He can't
see it. Poor old Delgas is so gentle and trusting that he
doesn't know how to look around the corner and see
the devil in what people do."

Silver smiled, his faint, faint smile. "As Wycombe lay
dying," he said, "there were three men in the world that
he wanted to kill. Name 'em, Delgas."

"You first, because you'd sunk a shot in him between
wind and water," said Delgas presently. "And I suppose
that me and Rutherford would come on the list, too."

"Very well," said Silver, "and to whom did he leave
his land?"

"Well, the same three. But how's he goin' to kill us by
givin' us the land?"

"Because he hoped that we'd not be friends. He hoped
that you and Rutherford would hang together and that
you'd be against me, and that we'd start a war and fight
to a finish."

"Hey!" exclaimed Delgas. "You mean that, Silver? You
think that's the straight of it, Harry?"

45

Harry Rutherford waved a slender hand.

"Of course that's it," he said. "Don't be so dumb, Brother Morris. Wycombe set us up for a battle royal. What else could he have had in his mind? Think that he wanted to *reward* us for being after his scalp?"

Delgas champed noisily on the butt of his cigar, the smoke squeezing out of the burning end of it in little rapid puffs.

"I begin to see," said he. "We can starve out Silver because we've got the land, and he can starve out us because he's got the water. The minute one shuts down on the other, there's bound to be trouble. It's a fight to the finish, and a mighty quick fight."

"There's only one way out," said Rutherford.

"Name it," said Delgas.

"Not to fight," said Rutherford.

"Sure! And that's easy," said Delgas. He turned to Silver. "You got a kind of an upstage way about you," he declared. "And maybe you ain't been very friendly toward the pair of us, now and then. But that don't matter to me so much. I can get on with anybody. My skin is thick enough. And I got a place in my system where I could use the dough we're goin' to pull down out of this business."

"So have I," said Rutherford. "All we need to do is to lay down a scheme to run the ranch. One of us has to run it, and the others stand by, and make a few suggestions."

"It won't work," said Silver.

"Why not?" asked Rutherford sharply.

Silver turned up the palm of his right hand.

"Do the same thing," he said to the others.

They obeyed him, frowning with curiosity.

"We've got soft hands," said Silver.

"Now, what the devil does that mean?" asked Delgas.

"Why, it means that we don't know enough about the

business to run a ranch, any of us," answered Rutherford shortly.

He left his chair and walked rapidly back and forth through the room. He seemed to be angry. Now and then he swore softly under his breath.

"Well," he exclaimed suddenly, stopping right in front of Silver, "what's the solution?"

"I haven't any," said Silver.

"What *have* you got, then?"

"Only an idea."

"Let's have it, Silver. Nobody accuses you of being a fathead. Fire away with the idea," urged Rutherford.

"My idea is that we all step out and let a fourth man run the place," suggested Silver.

"What man?" snapped Rutherford and Delgas in one voice.

"Any man we can all agree on," said Silver.

"Name one," said Rutherford.

"I haven't any names on the tip of my tongue," said Silver. "How about you?"

"It's all a funny business," said Delgas. "I dunno. I got no ideas. I only got a hunch that maybe Wycombe was right and a lot of trouble is likely to grow out of this here deal. Dead men don't enjoy the money they spend."

There was such truth in this remark that a short silence followed.

"How's the place running now?" demanded Rutherford.

"Pretty well, I suppose," said Silver. "The foreman knows his business. If he could suit a hound like Wycombe, he ought to suit us."

"There is something in that," agreed Delgas instantly.

"Make him the manager?" asked Rutherford.

"You fellows think that I'm sure to be against you, and that I'm sure to try to put one over on you," said Silver. "Get that idea out of your head. If you don't want

47

Farrel, take anybody you like—if I like him, too."

Delgas and Rutherford looked fixedly at one another.

"Well, that sounds all right to me," said Delgas.

Rutherford shrugged his narrow shoulders. He sat down, made a cigarette with the fingers of a conjurer, and lighted it. He spoke, breathing out the smoke through nose and mouth.

"Make it Farrel till we vote him out," suggested Rutherford. "A majority vote puts one ranch manager out and a new one in. This is a democratic country, and the majority ought to rule."

"You've got your voters all in a lump," answered Silver. "No. One vote has to be enough to put out the manager. And a new one can't go in until every one of the three of us is satisfied."

There was another silence.

"Well," said Rutherford, "that might mean never. We might never hit on the kind of a fellow who would please all of us. I'm for putting this whole ranch on sale and getting rid of it."

"You couldn't get a quarter of what it's worth," complained Delgas. "I asked a couple of bankers what this here place is worth. The money they talked made me sick, I can tell you! They don't want to pay nothing. Nothing at all! There ain't any market for desert land, like this. People are afraid of a big drought when even the well might go dry, and then the cows would starve before they could be drove to the nearest water hole. And all we could do would be to sell the cattle and call it quits. And I ain't ready to be robbed like that!"

"Nor I!" said Rutherford. He turned to Silver, saying: "We'll start out with Farrel, then. Your man Farrel will make a start. If any of us don't like him, he's fired on the spot. That suit you?"

"That has to suit," answered Jim Silver.

He stood up.

"You boys," he said, "have been talking about building a shack up in the foothills. You don't have to. You can stay right here and live in the house. It belongs to me, but you're mighty welcome to room in it."

He walked out of the room and into the kitchen, where he saw the girl. She had had sleepless nights since the death of Wycombe, and now there were black shadows inlaid around her eyes.

"It's all right," said Silver. "Farrel stays on. He's not the foreman, but the manager."

He went out to the place where Farrel was nailing some new shakes on the roof of the big shed. At the signal he gave, Farrel came quickly down to the ground.

"You're to stay on as manager," said Silver.

"Thanks," said Farrel. "I know you did that for me, Jim. It's not the first good thing you've done for me, though. Are things going to be all right?"

"All right?" echoed Silver, laughing a little. "Why, man, one of these days there's going to be an explosion big enough to blow up everything."

"Then why do you stay?" asked Farrel, agape. "Two of 'em to one of you. I'd be on your side, but I'm no gunman. Why do you stay, Jim?"

"Because," said Silver, "I don't know when the explosion will come, and I like to hear the fuse burn."

CHAPTER VIII
TROUBLE'S SIGN

Since Jim Silver looked for a storm, he was by no means deceived by the perfect peace and quiet of the first few days that followed, when big Morris Delgas and Harry Rutherford were both the perfection of consideration, as far as they knew how to be.

For one thing, they seemed to be taking very seriously their new-found duties as ranchers, for they were hardly ever at the ranch house, except for meals. The lunch hour they often missed completely when they went off on a whole day of exploration—"a day's hunt," as Morrie Delgas used to say, "to find mountain lions, mountain sheep, or mountain suckers."

Morrie Delgas was very gay. His loud voice boomed through the house. His heavy step thundered on the floor. Rutherford, beside him, was like a cat beside a horse, speaking little, keeping himself neat always, with a pale smile on his pale face. But, by the shifting lights in his eyes, it was plain that his mind was never still.

There was only one sign of trouble, a few days after Delgas and Rutherford came to live at the house. At the breakfast table, after Delgas had had his "eye opener" of rye, he boomed out to Silver:

"You've got the ready cash, Silver. You've got heaps

of it, and we're just about broke. How about a couple of thousand on account?"

Silver looked across the table and permitted his smile to broaden a trifle.

"You mean a couple of hundred, Morrie, don't you?" he asked.

Delgas stared back, not at Silver but at Rutherford.

"He says that I mean a couple of hundred, not grands," quoted Delgas.

Rutherford nodded. Nothing further was said, no gesture made to accept the money. Delgas seemed to be hearing what he expected, and Silver knew by a thrill in his bones that trouble had been brought still closer to him.

Two days later, Farrel reported quietly to Silver that he was beginning to have trouble with the men.

"They look me in the eye and swallow their grins," said Farrel. "I feel their eyes following me, too, and their grins when my back is turned."

"What's wrong?" asked Silver.

"You know," said Farrel, "one bad apple will spoil a barrel. And this gang was always a tough lot to handle. Wycombe wanted them that way. He never employed a man that hadn't done time."

"You mean all the lads on the place have a prison record of some sort?" asked Silver.

"That's what I mean," answered Farrel. "Wycombe always felt that he might get into a pinch where he'd want tough fellows around him, to back him up. So he collected this crew. Only, when he heard that both Delgas and Rutherford were on the trail after him, he lost his nerve and sent for you. He needed a bigger gun than any he'd ever hired, so he got hold of you. But there's not a man on the place that isn't pretty good with guns, in one way or another. Wycombe knew I hadn't been in jail, and that suited him because he wanted an honest foreman to handle accounts."

"How have you managed to handle this gang?" asked Silver curiously.

"I'm a little better with my hands than they are," said Farrel. "Besides, I know one end of a gun from another. They don't want trouble with me unless it's worth their while; but, if it *is* worth their while, any one of the lot would be glad enough to rip into me, I suppose."

"What bad apples were dropped into the barrel?" asked Silver.

"You guess," answered the foreman.

"You mean Delgas and Rutherford?"

"They're not too busy riding the range for the sake of hunting," said Farrel. "They never bring any game in. And they don't need all of this time to look over the lay of the land on the ranch. But I've spotted one of them time and again, off on the sky line, talking to one of the punchers and then fading out of the picture. They got up into the foothills, too. I don't know for what."

"Any guesses?" asked Silver.

"Yes. But nothing I can back on."

"Fire away."

"I think that they're in touch with crooks who'll buy a lot of cattle if they can get 'em at the right price. The other day I bumped into Sam Waring riding across our range. You know Sam?"

"No," said Silver.

He leaned back in his chair and let the sun flow over his body while his eyes were closed.

Farrel regarded the placid calm of his "one-third" boss with a troubled eye. He stepped closer as he added:

"Sam Waring is a tough hombre. He's as tough as they come. He's done plenty of time, and he's been up for counterfeiting. You know that they're tough when they handle the green goods."

52

"That's Federal business. Yes, they're tough or crazy when they handle the green goods," agreed Silver, opening his eyes drowsily.

"Waring," said Farrel, "isn't up here for his health. He's in on some deal or he wouldn't be around. He told me that he was just passing through on a line for the other side of the Farrel Mountains. But I think he was lying. He'd make a good running mate for Delgas and that ghoul of a Rutherford. If he's that close to them, it'll be strange if they don't get together."

"You don't like Rutherford?" said Silver.

"Do you?" asked Farrel.

"He's a handsome fellow," said Silver. "Go on and think out loud, Danny."

Farrel hesitated.

Then he exploded: "In two days the punchers on this place could sweep every sound head of cattle right off up the valleys in the foothills and turn 'em over to anybody with the cash to pay half value on the nail! And Waring always represents plenty of money. My hunch is that he's been sent for to take the cows—at a price."

"Why does this burn you all up?" asked Silver lazily.

"Why?" cried Farrel. "Because I've put in my years building the herd. When I came here, there was a scratch lot of worthless beef too weak to cover ground for fodder and get back to water again. I've traded and bred and fought and prayed to make this herd what it is. I came onto the job when I was a kid. I'm not very old now, but, believe me, I've done a lifetime's work already, I think.

"This herd is what it ought to be—long and rangy, with enough bone to carry flesh when the cattle go north to fatten on good grasslands. It's my work. It's the sort of a herd that used to run on the place when my father had the ground. You can't build the right sort of a herd in a minute. It takes years. Once it's wiped out, you have to go clear back to the start, and that's hard. Maybe you'll never hit just the right combination again. And now a pair of crooks are likely to wipe out all the work that I've done. That's why I'm burning up! That's why I want to know what you intend to do about it."

"Nothing," said Silver.

"Nothing?" cried Farrel.

"Not a thing—yet," said Silver.

"Then you're not worth the powder it would take to blow you up!" shouted Farrel.

Silver closed his half-opened eyes again.

Farrel's footsteps strode to the door and halted there.

"I've said too much," he growled. "You saved my hide, the other night. I forgot that for a minute. I remember it now. Silver, does it make any difference if I say I'm sorry?"

"Sure. It's all right," said Silver. "Don't worry about me. Just tell me why Delgas and Rutherford should want to sell all the stock off at about half price, will you?"

He kept his eyes closed, but he could feel young Farrel coming back toward him. The voice of the foreman grew louder, more vibrant again.

"Because," said Farrel, "if your share is thrown in with theirs and sold, they won't be losing so very much. Because fellows like that always prefer hard cash to anything else in the world. Finally, because, once the cattle are gone, they'll soon have *you* off the ranch—and they hate your heart. I've seen them looking at you when your back was turned. They hate your heart."

Silver, without opening his eyes, took a sack of tobacco out of a breast pocket, together with a little battered pack of wheat-straw papers. Deftly and blindly he made his cigarette, a trick very worthwhile to one who often must ride at night. He crimped one end of his smoke, put the other between his lips, took out a cube of sulphur

54

matches, and scratched one of them under the arm of his chair.

He allowed that match to burn for an instant so that the sulphur fumes would clear away. Then he lighted his cigarette and threw the match into the air. The flame fluttered out. The match left in the air a little irregular-curving streak of blue smoke. And still the eyes of Silver were not open as he smoked.

Farrel, biting his lips, took heed of all of these details.

"They want me out of the way?" said Silver. "How does having the cattle wangle that for them?"

"Don't you see?" argued the other. "That's your hold on them in this bargain about the leaving of the ranch?"

"I've got the house and the water rights."

"The house doesn't matter. And the water rights don't matter if there aren't any cattle to need the water. You'll be stuck here with nothing on your hands except the hard cash that you pulled down in the deal. You'll have no land; you'll have no cows; you'll have to clear out; and then they will manage to sell off the land. They'll pull the wool over the eyes of some fool of a tenderfoot buyer and make him think that he gets the water rights with the land. Isn't that clear?"

Silver whistled.

"I hadn't thought of all that," said he.

"And now," urged Farrel, "tell me what you're to do about it, will you?"

"I'm going to think," said Silver, and continued to smoke with closed eyes.

Farrel endured the picture of indifference as long as he could. Then he turned without a word and strode out of the room.

Silver continued to lead the life of an idler, rarely leaving the house. He was in bed early. He was up very late. As he sat alone at his breakfast, he could sometimes feel the eye of the girl fixed upon him with a melancholy appeal, but neither she nor Farrel spoke a word to him about the subject of Farrel's anxiety.

It was two days after this that the next step was made toward tragedy. Farrel came into the house in the middle of the day.

Through the window of his room, where he lounged in the easy-chair, Silver saw the foreman come from the corral with bowed head. In the kitchen, Farrel paused for a moment, and Silver heard the girl cry out sharply with pain.

By that, Silver knew what had happened. He knew still better when Farrel stood before him in the room, looking years older, wrinkled about the eyes, drawn, battered of face like one who has faced a great storm for many hours.

"Delgas and Rutherford have fired me," said Farrel. "They sent me to you for my pay."

CHAPTER IX
NINE AGAINST TWO

From the expression in the face of Silver, it seemed that he was hearing of a thing with which he had been long familiar.

He took out a wallet.

"What's owing?" he asked.

"I've had fifty from them. You owe me twenty-five."

Silver passed out the amount and replaced his wallet in his pocket. Farrel went back to the door and made a farewell speech.

"I thought it might be that we could make a fight to save the herd," he declared. "I thought you might be the one man in the world to beat those crooks. But I guess you're too tired. I'm thanking you for the life that I still walk around with—and—so long, Silver."

He was half through the doorway when Silver, his hands folded beneath his head, his eyes lazy, turned a little in the chair and asked:

"Where you going, Danny?"

"Going?" answered Danny. "I don't know. I don't care. Just somewhere."

"Why not stay here?"

"Here? I'm fired, I tell you. I've been paid off."

"You've been paid off by the ranch. Now I hire you again at the same rate of pay," said Silver.

At this, Farrel gripped the edge of the door so that

the knob of it jangled suddenly. Then he made a quick step back inside the room. He pulled the door shut as carefully as though death were in the making of a sound, and there he stood before Silver, staring with incredulous eyes.

"Sit down and rest your feet," said Silver.

"Tell me what's in the air?" asked Farrel.

"I'm retaining a good man because I might need him. You've got a room in the house. Go upstairs and use it."

"How?"

"Go up and lie down and rest."

"Rest? I don't need to rest."

"Do what I tell you," said Silver quietly. "There may be a time ahead when you won't rest for quite a spell. So long, Danny. Go take it easy while you can."

Farrel looked at him with blazing eyes. "I might have known," he said, with a trembling voice. "I might have known that you wouldn't lie down and take it—like a dog! I don't care what pops. I'm with you to the finish." He went out of the room. The keen ear of Silver, afterward, heard the excited babbling of voices in the kitchen, and he smiled.

Delgas and Rutherford came in before supper time, and Delgas said carelessly: "That bum of a Dan Farrel, I gave him the rush to-day. He's no good."

"He's a tramp," said Rutherford.

Silver, reclined in his chair, looked over the two of them casually. The face of Rutherford, which generally was the color of a cellar-grown plant, was now patched with sunburn, and his lips were gray from the chapping wind raised by a galloping horse. Dust had reddened the eyes of both men. Delgas had fortified his greasy skin by letting a week's beard darken his face. They sat down uninvited in the room of Silver and lighted cigars.

"Not much cow sense—Farrel?" asked Silver gently.

"Cow sense? No sense at all," said Delgas. "I been

58

watching him. I been out and around, since I came onto this place. You been layin' low and takin' things easy. That's all right if it's your way, but I mean to make a real ranch out of this dump. Know that, Jim?"

"I'm glad of that," said Silver.

"I even got Harry Rutherford interested," said Delgas. "He thinks that some of my ideas are pretty good, eh, Harry?"

Rutherford shrugged his shoulders. He sat on the base of his spine and inhaled the strong smoke of the cigar and then blew it in a swift stream high toward the ceiling.

"What we gotta do is use some brains," said Delgas. "That's what we gotta do. And I'll tell you the trouble with Farrel. Know what it is?"

"Well?" said Silver.

"No brains," said Delgas. "Eh, Harry?"

"No brains," said Rutherford.

"I'm sorry about that," said Silver. "He looks to me like a decent sort."

"Yeah. Clean hands," said Delgas. "Yeah, clean hands and a washout for a brain, eh, Harry?"

"Washout," said Harry Rutherford, coldly, to the ceiling.

"Just a dumb kind of an hombre," said Delgas. "It's lucky that we been out and watched him workin' the men. That's the main trouble. The men don't care a thing about him. Eh, Harry?"

"Not a thing," said Rutherford.

"He looks like something," went on Delgas, clearing his throat, "and he stands like something, and he sticks out his chest like something. But he ain't nothing at all. He's a blank. So we gave him the bum's rush. Just thought we'd tell you, though."

"Thanks," said Silver. He made a cigarette in his unconcerned way.

"You're having a rest, Silver, eh?" said Rutherford, suddenly curious. "From what I knew about you, I thought you were the sort of an hombre that never ran dry, never got out of patience, never knew what it was to quit. That all wrong?"

"I only do what I have to do," said Silver, smiling.

Rutherford was sitting straight up, his eyes lighted with keen concentration, a focused brilliance.

"You're different from what I thought," admitted Harry Rutherford.

"Sorry," said Silver, still smiling.

Rutherford's eyes were darkened by a frown.

"Unless you're putting on a front for me," said Rutherford.

"Aw, quit tryin' to get behind everything," protested Delgas, pulling out a flask and putting it to his lips for a long swig. "You take a bird like Harry, that's got brains, and the trouble with him is that he's always trying to use 'em. Know that? Never contented. Always got to keep hammerin' away at people. Give a gent a chance to rest, will you, Harry?"

"Shut up, will you?" answered Rutherford softly. And still he peered at Silver and at the steady, dull-eyed smile with which Silver looked back at him.

Suddenly Rutherford rose, went to the door, paused there, and finally left the room.

Delgas looked after him, his grin gradually widening on both sides of his cigar, his brown-stained lips shining with the juice from the tobacco.

"Funny, ain't he?" he said to Silver. "He's got something in his head, has that bird Rutherford. He *is* like a bird—just like a bird, always cocking his head around and looking at something. He don't give you no peace, not when you're his partner. Now I tell you what— I gotta go and corral him and find out what's made him so shifty on his pins, all at once. See you later, brother."

He in turn paused at the door.

"You paid off your third to Farrel?" he asked.

"I paid him," said Silver.

"Good riddance," said Delgas. "Cheap at twice the price, I say." He was smiling more broadly than ever as he turned and left the room.

Before supper time, as Silver lay quietly in his chair and watched the evening rise like blue water among the canyons of the mountains, Farrel tapped at the door and came in again. He said uneasily:

"There's going to be an explosion if I walk into that dining room after the pair of them have fired me off the place."

"Well," said Silver, couching his big head in his hands again, "there's got to be an explosion some time, and you've had a long rest, this afternoon."

Farrel went to the window and looked out as though something had suddenly taken his eyes, but Silver knew that he was looking at nothing but the sweetness of life. It might well be that both of them were hardly an hour from the end of everything.

"There has to be a show-down," said Silver.

"You told 'em that you'd keep me on?"

"No," said Silver, and watched his man wince. Farrel stepped back from the window and turned a gray face to Silver.

"What's the good?" he asked. "Seven and two make nine. There's nine of 'em. Nine against two. That's not funny."

"No, that's not funny," said Silver lazily, yawning out the words.

Farrel suddenly pointed a hand at him and said: "I think you like this sort of a business! It's fun, for you."

61

"I don't know," said Silver. "It just has to be done. That's all."

Farrel cleared his throat, made a turn through the room, confronted that placid face again.

"Two men can't kill nine. Not nine like them. Not in a closed room. There's no chance."

"There's no chance," said Silver, nodding.

"Then what the devil?" demanded Farrel.

"We've got to keep the devil out, I'd say. Keep the devil out of their heads and the guns out of their hands."

"How?"

"You come in after everybody else has sat down. Will you do that?"

Farrel drew a long breath. His right hand doubled into a fist and then slowly relaxed again.

"Yes," he said slowly. "I'll come in—after everybody else is at the table."

"Good boy," said Silver. "You'll be heeled, eh?"

"I've got a gun. So have all the rest of those tramps."

"Carry two guns, and then you'll be one up on some of them."

"I thought you said the thing was for us to keep this from coming to a fight?"

"I did," answered Silver. "But if the fighting starts, we want to scratch them up a little, eh? We want to make a few dents."

"Silver," murmured the other, "we may both be dead men, in half an hour!"

"We certainly may," said Silver. "But there has to be a show-down, or else they're apt simply to pick us up and throw us off the ranch. If they once have us on the run, they'll keep us there."

Farrel looked out the darkening window and muttered: "Well, it's better than chucking in our hand. I'll walk in—with two guns on me. And then?"

"Well," said Silver, "after that we'll have to watch the

play of the cards. That's all. Just see how they fall."

Farrel smiled a twisted smile, saying: "And follow the lead?"

Silver sat up and suddenly caught the hand of the cow-puncher.

"That's it, Danny," he said. "Play all your cards—and follow the lead!"

CHAPTER X

THE SHOW-DOWN

Trouble was so thick in the air of the dining room, that night, that the girl seemed to sense it long before the men came in. Perhaps she had been watching their faces through the window, and listening to their voices. At any rate, she had a sick, pale face when Silver walked through the kitchen as the gong sounded. She stood back with a great platter of corn bread to let him pass, and her frightened eyes turned up silently to his face.

"What's the matter, Esther?" he asked her.

She shook her head.

"Say it," persuaded Silver. "It's better to talk a thing out."

"What will happen?" she breathed, with a tremor of hysteria in her voice. "What will they do to Danny—and you?"

"What does Danny think?"

"He hasn't said anything. But I know he was fired, and that you took him on again. You don't think—"

"Everything is going to be all right," said Silver. "Enough has happened in that dining room already. It ought to be peaceful the rest of its life."

He walked on into the dining room, where there was a great scuffling of feet and groaning of chair legs as the punchers took their places. One thing was instantly noticeable: Delgas sat at the top of the table, which hitherto had been Silver's place, not because he had any essential right to that chair but because the weight of his name was greater than the repute of either of the other owners of the ranch. Now Delgas was there, squaring his great shoulders.

Silver went down toward the foot of the table and took a vacant chair. Delgas looked at him flat in the eye, saying:

"Turn and turn about, eh, Jim? I thought I'd try the fit of this place."

All eyes flashed toward Silver. When they saw him merely smile, one of the men burst out with loud laughter. He choked it off suddenly.

It was Red, who was in the act of hanging his sombrero on a peg of the wall; now he changed his mind and put the hat on the back of his head before he sat down. He sat a little sidewise, as though he were ready to talk rather than to eat. And his mischievous, bright eyes went back and forth across the other faces around him.

The clatter of the crockery and the clashing of the knives and forks had begun in another moment when tall Dan Farrel walked quietly through the door.

"Hey! There's the big stiff now!" shouted a puncher.

Farrel got to the vacant chair which had not been noticed before. He was pale. He wore a wooden, brittle smile that made Silver bite his lip. For, without help, he knew that he could never win through the scene that was to come.

All the banter had disappeared from the eyes of the men about the table, as they saw Farrel sitting down. Rutherford looked straight at Silver, and seemed to wait. It was Delgas who heaved himself to his feet and bellowed:

"You bum, you ain't wanted. Get out of that chair!

65

You're fired. Get off the ranch, you namby-pamby blockhead! You ain't wanted. Get out before I throw you out!"

"I'm hired again," said Farrel, with a barely audible voice. He cleared his throat.

"Hired? You lie!" yelled Delgas, throwing his head from side to side. "You lie and you lie loud! Who hired you again?"

"Jim Silver," said Farrel, sitting stiffly erect on the edge of his chair.

The words struck a silence through the room. Every man at the table stirred a little, and all eyes centered on Silver, as though Farrel no longer existed.

"You?" called Delgas in a mighty voice. "You hired that fool again?"

"You know, Morrie," said Silver, "that what's a fool to you might be a wise man to me. We don't all want the same things."

Delgas looked aside at Rutherford, but Rutherford stared only at Silver, like a hungry cat. He was not paler. He was simply set and ready. Silver folded his arms. He smiled straight back at Delgas.

"We don't want the same things, eh?" said Delgas. "I wanta know what there is around here that you'd like to change?"

The arms of Silver unfolded, and two oversized Colts winged in his hands. One of them pointed at Rutherford. With the left-hand gun he shot the hat off the head of Red.

From the corner of his eye he saw that two guns were now in the hands of Farrel, and he breathed more easily. With that backing, he might win.

Out of the kitchen came a scream, and Silver surmised that the girl was watching through the dining-room doorway. Rutherford sat with his right hand deep beneath his coat, motionless. He had been fully prepared, and yet he was a thousandth part of a second too late, and knew it. Delgas, too, had flung a hand back to his hip and kept it there. Not a man at the table that had failed to make a move toward a gun, only to have the firing of the shot make each one realize that he was too late and that he, perhaps, would be the next target.

As for Red, he had ducked his head forward and looked at Silver as if at a hangman who was about to drop the trap.

All of this Silver saw by the time the hat of Red had flown into the air, struck the wall, and flopped loudly against the floor. All noises were loud now. With a little care, one could distinguish the breathing of every man at the table.

"One thing I'll change at the start," said Silver, "is the wearing of hats at the table. The second thing I'll change is cursing out any man that works for me. Delgas, watch yourself!"

For the shoulder of Delgas had twitched a little.

"All right," said Morris Delgas in a barely audible voice.

Silver stood up slowly. If he made a swift move, he knew that every man at the table would grab at a gun. So he rose slowly. He seemed to be watching everybody, but in reality he had his eye on Delgas and Rutherford only. Rutherford, he knew, was his chief care. However formidable Delgas might be as a great brute of a man, he was nothing compared to the catlike speed and surety of Rutherford.

"Stand up, Farrel," commanded Silver. "Start at the end of the table with Delgas and go around the line. See how much hardware you can collect and pile it on the floor."

"If you do that—" began Rutherford, and then stopped himself. He was pale enough now. All the heat and color of his body had gone into his eyes as he stared at Silvertip, and Jim Silver knew that before the end of the

67

game one of the two of them would have to die. This moment in the dining room was only the first trick. Others would inevitably follow.

"I'm going to do that," said Silver. "Start in, Danny. I'll try to entertain the rest of you boys while you wait. Go slow and be sure, Danny. We ought to collect quite a lot of valuable stuff, this way. Anybody would be glad to see it—a sheriff particularly. Now, the rest of you fellows, I know that you're only a lot of cheap rats. You've followed Rutherford and Delgas, and you've burned your fingers with the first trick. Other tricks are going to come. Perhaps I'll have a chance to see the lot of you dead or jailed as a pack of dirty cattle rustlers and horse thieves. I don't know; I'm just hoping. Keep your hands on the table; make no quick moves; and you can start eating as soon as you've let Danny take a weight off your mind."

Farrel had reached a long-drawn, lean-faced cow-puncher who said gently:

"I'm goin' to cut your heart out for this, Farrel."

Farrel said nothing. He went on with his collection. There was not a man at the table who carried less than one revolver. A good many had knives, also. The collection went on gradually.

"Come down here and take my place," said Silver. "Down here, Delgas. I thought you might fit at the head of the table, but I see you're not man enough."

Delgas, breathing like a steam engine, walked silently down the room.

"I ain't hungry," he said. "I'm goin' to go outside."

"To get a rifle and start shooting through the door?" asked Silver, smiling. "No; wait a while, and maybe your appetite will come back."

Delgas took the vacated place where Silver had been sitting. The man seemed to be suffering from a fit that contracted the muscles of his body and twisted his face into a horror. He was insane with a rage which he dared not express in action, but his hands gripped the edge of the table so hard that his arms shuddered with the might of that grasp.

When the crew had been disarmed thoroughly, from first to last, Silver said:

"Some of you boys may have a decent streak in you. If you have, stay in the room after the rest go out. That's all. I can use a right man who thinks that he can use me. Now those of you who want to finish supper, stay right in your places. The rest of you can file out. Danny, pull down the blinds of those windows and watch the door."

He paused. Every man arose. Only Red seemed to find it hard to get out of his chair, as he kept his fascinated eyes upon the face of Silver. But Delgas, in passing, spoke one word to him, and Red nodded and followed.

They went out the door with Rutherford, as might have been expected, the last one through—a rear guard to see that the rest did the right thing for him.

For his own part, he turned and bowed to Silver, a little, short jerk of head and body, as though he were acknowledging an introduction.

"Silver, you're quite a fellow," he said. "When the time comes for the finish of you, it ought to be a party I'll want to remember. So long!"

And he stepped out into the dark of the night.

CHAPTER XI

BESIEGED

Routed troops need a time for rallying, even if they have fallen back without loss. After the sinister face of Rutherford had disappeared from the doorway, the two men and the girl inside the house could hear the scattering of voices drawing gradually together, increasing in loudness. It left one moment for consultation to the three.

Silver, as he turned toward the frightened girl, saw that she was carrying a double-barreled shotgun that dragged down her arm with its weight. But, no matter how white her face or how big her eyes, it was clear that she was not near fainting. She had meant business with that powerful weapon so long as her lover was in danger.

Tall Dan Farrel locked the door swiftly. As he turned, he was saying:

"Silver, if we get into the kitchen side of the house, we could stand a siege, maybe. They're not through with us. There are other guns they'll get their hands on. This heap isn't all that they have. They'll come back at us."

Silver was gathering the weighty heap of revolvers; he let the big knives lie.

"You're right," he told Farrel. "They may try to rush us, but I doubt it. There's no use in trying to watch all sides of the house. We can't do it. Better get into the

70

kitchen and wait there. It has windows looking on two sides."

What he said was law. They got into the kitchen, locked and braced chairs against the doors from it leading into the dining room and the main body of the house, and hastily threw open the windows to either side and the kitchen door which faced the big shed.

For, as Silver said, it was necessary for them to look out on the ground nearby. The lamp in the kitchen was out. The girl sat in a chair against the wall, facing the stove. Silver had for his province the window and door toward the big corral. Farrel had the surveillance of the opposite window.

Farrel sat in a chair near the window with a rifle across his knees. Silver lay flat on the floor with another rifle beside him. The girl still kept her double-barreled shotgun. If it came to a sudden rush, that weapon might do more execution than a dozen rifles. Silver expected no mass attack simply because there was little practical value behind such a move. It would gratify the spite of the offended men, but it would put no hard cash into the pockets of their leaders.

Inside, a big-lidded kettle was muttering and hissing on the stove, from which red pencils of light flowed through the darkness. But the outer night was more fully illumined. Silver could see the upward flow of the mountains against the northern stars, and the gaunt legs of the windmill, and the great, rounded mass of the iron tank which seemed suspended in the air without support. He could make out portions of the fence, also, and guess at the position of the two haystacks. The shed itself was, of course, clearly discernible as to the roof, but the rest of it merged toward the shadows of the ground. It seemed easier to look into the distance and make out the objects near the horizon than to study things close at hand.

71

There seemed to be a motion of the ground toward the house. The surface seemed to be pouring slowly toward his watchful eyes.

He tried his rifle sights at big objects and small. He drew a bead on the wavering streak of a fence post, even; but the star sheen along the barrel troubled him a little. He went to the stove, got some of the blacking on his fingers, and smeared that along the top of the rifle barrel. He went back and lay down.

"If they put fire to the house—" said the girl.

"Silence!" commanded Silver.

She was quiet. Farrel cleared his throat softly, very softly.

Out of the distance, now, they heard outbreaks of loud, arguing voices. These noises were interspersed with moments of silence; there followed a considerable time when not a sound was heard except from the windmill. A breeze was turning the wheel slowly; at intervals the stream from the pump dropped. The water in the tank was so low that the water fell like a hand on a brazen drum, with splashings and reverberations. This noise seemed to grow louder and louder. Sometimes it was as if the windmill and tank were moving toward the house. Silver kept on taking sights at everything he could see, making his vision small enough to grasp the least possible targets.

Then a tumult broke out in the dining room. The door went down with a crash—that door, it seemed, which communicated with the outside. Footfalls boomed on the floor. A ray of light worked fitfully around the edges of the door that closed the kitchen away from the dining room. A hand shook that door. Silver promptly put a bullet high up through the woodwork.

He had fired high on purpose. To shoot even at hostile men with nothing but blind chance to guide the bullet

72

was against his nature, and the force of necessity had little control over his instincts. But, though he purposely had fired the warning shot high, a yell of derision came from the men in the next room. There seemed to be three or four of them, at least. Their footfalls rapidly retreated; they made no further effort, for the moment, to get into the kitchen.

After that, a portion of them, at least, were heard leaving the dining room. Perhaps one man was left there as a guard and spy to hem in the maneuvers of the three.

Silver saw a dim silhouette of a man move out toward the big corral and the shed. Another and another stealthy figure followed. Parade was out there in the shed, either munching hay or lying down at ease. Parade was there, but Silver would not fire at the unknown men on account of any hope of preserving the stallion. He had, in fact, a strong hope that the horse would be able to preserve himself.

Then Farrel fired a shot. The boom of the gun was thunderous in the small kitchen. It seemed to bring a jingling echo out of the iron-work of the stove. Outside, there was silence. Then voices stirred far away at the horse shed, followed by an outcry of curses at the farther end of the house.

"I missed that one, all right," Farrel said. "I won't miss the next, I hope."

They heard doors flung open, and heavy feet trampling across floors. At last there were men in the next room, where Silver had lounged all those recent days.

Someone bawled out: "We got you! We know you're in the kitchen. We're goin' to blow you to pieces, Silver! We're goin' to smear you all over the place."

Silver said nothing.

He could make out the rumbling voice of Delgas saying: "This is where the hound has been takin' it easy.

This is where he's been sleepin' away his days. Oh, ain't he goin' to eat his heart—ain't he eatin' it now, to think what a fool we've made of him?"

One of the others laughed. Someone burst out in a tirade. Silver got up and went quietly to the door that opened on this room. He began to move away, silently, the chairs that were braced against it.

Then the girl reached for him and found him in the darkness. "Don't do it! Don't do it!" she said.

"What?" whispered Silver.

"You want to throw that door open and sweep them out of the house. Don't do it, Jim. Please don't go mad!"

He realized that he *was* mad, that an overmastering hunger to destroy them like reptiles had made a blackness of his brain. He put the chair soundlessly back in place and went back to lie on the floor at the door.

Some day, he knew, he would be led to throw his life away by the headlong sweeping of one of those fighting impulses of his that throttled his good sense and judgment. He grew afraid, as he lay there, not of all the danger that lay in the outer night but of himself. He began to forget the whole situation and wonder about himself; but all the while he was as alert as a wild cat hunting over strange ground.

From the horse shed came a crashing and snorting.

It raised him to his feet. The girl was beside him again, with her hand on his arm. He struck it away and strode for the door. She gripped him again.

"They're waiting for you to go out, when you hear Parade!" she warned him. "They're watching this door and the window, hoping that you'll come out. They're watching from each side, I know. They want to murder you, Jim!"

He thought of the soft gold of Parade and of the flexible steel that underlay the surface; he thought of the great wise brain of the stallion and the heart without fear. He began to tremble. The girl's hands kept pulsing against him, not strongly, but with a steady rhythm.

"No," he whispered at last. "I won't go. I'm ashamed. I'm only a fool and a baby. And you see through me. But I won't go."

He made himself get down on one knee, and then she went back to her place against the wall.

"She's the captain, the leader, the brain, and I'm only a pair of blind hands working by direction," he told himself.

He began to see her with clearness. He saw her more clearly in the darkness than ever he had seen her before in the light of the day, for he could place his memory on every bit of her.

She wore rubber gloves to keep her hands from puffing and reddening in the dishwater, but nevertheless, potatoes and onions and the handling of meat had stained her skin. Her hands were small and well-made but they were not pretty. Hands of a woman ought to be smooth and brown; they don't need to be very little, but the skin should be perfectly kept, thought Silver. And her hands would never be right because all her life she would be working away at sewing or cooking or scrubbing floors. She got right down on her knees and went after a floor with might and main. He had seen her making the suds fly. She scrubbed a floor white, like the deck of a ship. And if she were not doing work like that for a husband, she would surely be doing it for hire.

Silver decided, suddenly, that it was the matter of her hands that kept her from being beautiful, in his eyes. Her face was well enough. And her eyes were a blue stain in it. When she looked at Silver, her eyes and her mouth were still with awe; when she looked at Farrel, a smile kept dawning and dying on her lips and eyes. She kept taking gentle possession of him with her glances.

It might be a woman something like that who would

one day, for the first time, fling open the door to Silver's heart and walk in and take command. Men said that when the moment came, they were helpless. They resisted, they fought against the thing, they fled from it. But they always fled in a circle and came back to the starting point. He would be like all the rest—one day!

Out of the shed figures moved again. A door opened with a crash.

"Ride him, cowboy! Ride him!" yelled a chorus of voices.

He heard the brazen neigh of Parade. It made him think of days of long ago when he had followed the great horse across the endless desert. That neigh had been the challenge that rung in his ears in those times until by chance and fortune and kindness, more than strength, at last he made the great horse his own. But it was not possession. He belonged to Parade as much as Parade belonged to him.

Now he was fighting against the mastery of another man, out there in the darkness. Silver heard the thumping of the hoofs on the ground, then a form exploded upward, vaguely spread-eagled against the horizon stars.

"Get the rope! Hold him! That's it!" shouted voices. "Now, Rutherford, if you can ride anything that wears hair, you take your turn!"

They might wear down Parade among them, taking him turn after turn. A whistle trilled suddenly out of the mouth of Silver. It brought as an echo a wild tumult, an outcrying. A gun barked, and another weapon spat fire. Then a mighty form winged over the corral fence.

Silver stood up, and called. Right to the kitchen door raced Parade, skidded to a halt, then entered, crouched low, feeling his way over the sagging, creaking boards, with bended legs. Like a monstrous cat shuddering on unknown ground, surrounded by the fear of traps, the big horse entered to the voice of Silver. At another word

76

he lay down. His great breathing filled the room. The shouting outside was a dim and vague and distant thing to Silver, as he ran his hand over the body of the stallion, feeling for blood.

He found nothing. Blood was not running onto the floor, either. The hand which gripped the heart of Silver gradually relaxed. He drew his hand slowly over the face of the horse, reading the features of it with well-remembering finger tips. Then he went back to lie down at guard in the doorway again.

Out by the shed, men were cursing, blaming one another. And Silver began to laugh, a mere soundless vibration in the darkness.

For toward the east he saw the gleam of an increasing pyramid of light on the horizon and he knew that before long the moon would be riding above the desert. The instant its bright rim was up, all of those men would be in peril around the ranch house, and they must know it by this time. A very little longer and they probably would withdraw.

CHAPTER XII

FARREL'S DECISION

The most alarming outburst of all came afterward. Perhaps it was the loss of the great horse that maddened the gang, but suddenly in the house broke out a great crashing and smashing as if men with axes were breaking all they could put their hands on. Voices came into the next room and bawled out curses. Other voices shouted in triumph as various bits of loot were found.

And then Rutherford was saying in his calm way: "You've won the second round, too, Silver. But the end of the fight hasn't come yet. Something tells me that I'm going to have the killing of you, Jim, and ride your horse afterward."

Although he did not lift his voice, he seemed to be speaking right there in the kitchen beside Silver. It was an uncanny thing. It sent strange shudders of apprehension through the body of Silver.

After that, the gang withdrew. In the distance behind the corral there were noises of the snorting horses as they were saddled and bridled. A few loud whoops were raised by the chorus, and after that they heard the beat of the departing hoofs.

Silver went out first, made a tour around the house, and then through the darkness of all the rooms inside it. For it was not impossible that a man or two might have been left behind to take him by surprise after he had counted on the retreat of the entire body. However, he found nothing except the smashed furniture and the ruined rooms where the thugs of Rutherford and Delgas had wreaked their angry disappointment.

It was only after he had completed his tour that Silver came back into the kitchen, called Parade into the open with a word, and gave permission for the kindling of a light. He asked for bacon and corn bread and coffee. He gave one glance at the girl and her sweetheart, their faces still pale and set from the ordeal that had been passed. Then he said:

"I'm going outside to have another look around and try to think out the next step. Whatever it is, you'll probably have to ride with me and leave Esther behind. Say good-by before I get back. That is, if you still want to see this business through, Farrel."

He went outside and watched the rising of the moon as it puffed out its swollen yellow cheeks and then, climbing higher in the sky, drew into a smaller, brighter sphere of silver. It was one of those nights when a man thinks that he can see not the flatness of the disk but the roundness of the orb. As Silver watched the progress of the moon, he saw it strike a cloud into transparent spray and emerge on the farther side, sweeping along as though a stronger wind were in that billowing, bright sail.

He could not help wondering what that moon would see of him before the sun came up to turn its brilliance into no more than a pale-azure cloud in the Western sky. Delgas, and the crowd of punchers who had all done time, and above all, the pale, thoughtful face of Rutherford—they would have to be encountered, perhaps, before this single night had ended.

He went back, finally, into the kitchen, and as he entered, he heard young Dan Farrel laughing with the girl. The smoke and steam of cookery made a bright mist in the room. He felt a tang of appetite greater than he had

79

known for a week. The anxiety since the supper gong sounded had been like a day's labor to build hunger.

They sat together, the three of them, while the stallion wandered back and forth outside, now and then putting his head through the doorway to watch his master, recoiling again because of the offensive smell of cooked meat and steaming coffee.

"He'd rather have oats," said the girl. "I'll get him an apple. Will he eat apples?"

Silver said vaguely: "I remember a time when he ate raw meat. Raw meat, wrapped up in fat, and stuffed down his throat. He ate a lot of it. He ate nothing else for four days—and he kept on going!"

"On a diet of meat?" cried Farrel, agape. "How did that happen? In a desert somewhere?"

"Pretty much in a desert. Away down south in Mexico, where the mountains are all scalped and where the sun burns the grass down to the roots Sometimes I found a cactus and pared the thorns off of it and shredded the fibers and gave some of that to Parade, too. It was filthy stuff. It was like offering him dry rope. But he'll eat anything in a pinch. He ran wild, you know, and wild horses know the point of eating or dying. Parade will always eat!"

"What was happening?" asked the girl. "Had you just got lost in the desert? How terrible!"

"Lost?" said Silver, more vaguely than before. "Well, that's one way of putting it. I had to be lost to the eyes of a lot of hombres who were riding after me."

"After you? But they never caught up with you?"

Silver looked at her with a very faint and very grim smile.

"Yes," he said. "Some of them caught up with me, too. But after a time that gang stopped following and turned back."

"All that were left of 'em?" suggested Farrel eagerly.

"Well," said Silver, as he finished eating and confined his attention to coffee, "there's still a job ahead. Farrel, you don't own a hair of a cow or an acre of land in the deal. Do you still want to ride with me?"

"I do," said Farrel.

Silver looked at the girl.

"Do you think that he ought to?" asked Silver.

She kept looking at Silver with great eyes of fear while she reached out for Farrel and blindly found him. Then as her hand tightened on him, she said:

"Yes. I think he ought to go."

"You've made up your mind?" asked Silver.

"I'd rather," said she, and paused, but went on again: "I'd rather remember him dead in a way like that—than dodging."

Silver said nothing. He began to frown into his coffee. It was almost unprecedented in his life. He had been with plenty of men who were willing to fight most desperately, but always because they had as great a goal as he, or a greater one. It was a novelty to him to find a fellow who was willing to throw himself away out of friendship, or gratitude for a past service.

Perhaps he should not permit that sacrifice. And yet he had in mind a reward that would repay Farrel for every effort, in the end. There was a battle to fight, first, and in that battle the odds were exactly nine to two— unless Sam Waring and perhaps sundry others were enlisted in the fight before the end.

He made a cigarette, lighted it, and tried to see the right course more clearly through the smoke.

"You talk, Farrel," he commanded suddenly. "You tell me what we ought to do."

"Go to town," said Farrel. "That's the best way, and get a whole mob of gunmen to come out here and mop up the thugs."

"How far to town?" asked Silver.

81

"Ten hours, I suppose."

"And then two or three hours, anyway, to get together enough of the right sort of men and mount them. Another ten hours to get back. That's one day."

Farrel nodded, frowning.

"It won't do," said the girl.

"Why not?" asked Farrel. "It's the best thing that we can do."

"What will Rutherford do now?" asked Silver of the girl.

She made a sweeping gesture.

"He'll have the men clear off the whole place. He'll have them clear off every cow on the place and all the horses. Every head of live stock will be up there in the foothills, somewhere, within four or five hours. Because Danny says that the men have been drifting everything north for days. They have them ready, now, for a quick push."

Silver nodded. "That's what Rutherford will do," he agreed.

Farrel looked painfully down at the table, before he began to shake his head.

"You're right," he said. "There's not time enough to let us get to town and back. There never was time enough for that. There's only the pair of us against the nine of them—plus a lot of others that we don't know anything about!"

He took a good swallow of coffee. The girl was watching him with a peculiar anxiety. Silver watched him, too. Farrel was no lover of danger. That was clear. But he had two senses. One was of honor and one was of duty. They pinched and whitened his face, but at last he was able to lift his head.

"All right," he said quietly to Silver. "I didn't see, at first, just what I was heading for. Now I see and I'll go through with it if I can."

"You know the lay of the land," said Silver. "What ought we to do, Danny?"

Farrel brushed his knuckles across his forehead and left three parallel streaks of white from the greatness of the pressure.

He flung out a hand behind him, pointing north.

"They'll scoop 'em all up and throw 'em into one of the two valleys," he declared. "They'll sweep 'em into the gap between the foothills of the Farrel Mountains and the hills below Mount Humphreys. Or else they'll drive through between the Humphreys Mountains and the Kendal Hills. That's the easiest way."

Silver nodded. "After that?" he suggested.

"Well," said Farrel slowly, as though he were willing to let his mind dwell on the details, "after that they'll have no trouble. They'll split the big herd into little sections and wind 'em through the mountains. You can depend upon it, if I'm right and they're ready to make their sale, somewhere up there in the mountains there are a lot of punchers ready to grab the herd for Sam Waring and push it away to markets that we don't know anything about. You could sprinkle ten million cows through those mountains and make it hard for anything but hawks to find 'em!"

"That's what they'll do then," said Silver calmly. "I believe every word that you say. But what about the pair of us? What can we do to stop 'em?"

Farrel stirred uneasily in his chair.

"Well," he said at last, "I don't know. First, we'll have to spot the way they're taking. That means that we'll have to separate. You go to the head of the valley between Humphreys and Kendal. I'll go to the head of the valley between Humphreys and Farrel Mountain. The one who sees the drift of cattle coming can climb the high hill at the foot of Humphreys. Know that hill?"

"No."

"You'll spot it easily enough. It stands up like a spur, all by itself. A fire lighted on that hill can be seen in both valleys. It will be the call which tells the other fellow that he's wanted. And when the herd comes—and you and I are both together—well, then Heaven alone can tell what we'll be able to do!"

CHAPTER XIII

THE SIGNAL FIRE

It was not so much the courage of Farrel that moved Silver, though it was a stirring thing to see the way the man drove his unwilling mind, as it was the strength of the girl. Not once did she falter.

The horses had been cleared out of the big corral, as a matter of course, by the retiring men of Rutherford and Delgas. But there were others in more distant fields. Silver went out on Parade and daubed a rope on a strong-looking mustang that led its herd in the effort to escape but could not lead fast enough to run away from the devouring stride of Parade. He brought that horse back and saddled it while Farrel said good-by to the girl.

She was as steady as a rock, saying good-by. Silver, when he took her hand, said:

"You have to stay alone, here, and I know that's hard to do. You have to let Dan go with me. And that's harder still. You're a brick, and I'm not forgetting it."

That was all. He made her no promises of reward because he felt that such talk would be an insult to a spirit like hers. Then he rode off at the side of Farrel. They were well-armed, well-mounted, and they had their wits about them. But as they got under way and as the outlines of the foothills drew nearer to them under the brightness of the moonlight, the thing looked more and more hopeless to Silver.

Farrel drew up his horse presently and pointed off to the right.

"That's your way, Jim," said he. "Ride up the valley there between the foothills. When you get to the head of it, you can wait. If my idea's right, those punchers are sweeping in the cows right now, out of the desert behind us. Once they get the herd together and start it rolling, it will move fast because these cows can run and keep on running like horses. They can be pushed like a big gang of mustangs. You'll hear 'em coming before you see 'em, maybe. And when you hear 'em pointing up your valley, climb the hill that will be off to the side—you won't miss it—and light the fire. If I don't see the red of the fire in this moonlight, I'll spot the rising of the smoke. Is that all straight?"

"That's all straight," said Silver. Then he added:

"I'd very much like to know the top thing in your mind, right now."

"Why," said Farrel, "I'm thinking about Steve Wycombe. Wherever he is, if he knows what's happening on earth, he must be laughing. See the way it's all working out for him! He split up his land among three men, and now he's got a first-rate chance that they'll cut each other's throats for the sake of his land. He's got a ten-to-one chance that *you'll* go down, anyway. And you're the one that bumped him off. Oh, Steve's laughing good and hard now, all right."

Silver nodded. "Let him laugh," he murmured. "One chance in ten isn't bad, when the stakes run high. Every man bets on a long shot, now and then. That's the spice of life."

Farrel stared back at him. Silver could feel the eyes under the black mask of shadow that fell across the forehead of his companion.

"I'd like to know one thing, Jim," said Farrel. "What's the top layer in *your* mind, just now?"

"The white of Rutherford's face," said Silver instantly. "And the blue of the eyes of your girl. I hope that you get back to her. But—so long, Danny!"

He shook hands with Farrel, and saw the puncher jog his mustang off to the left until it was out of sight beyond the first of the low-rolling hills that descended from the mighty knees of Mount Humphreys.

It was a bitter business, and he wondered how he could be justified by any sense of higher right in allowing this man to ride into the danger. Yet something sure and strong in the nature of Silver told him that he was right. If all worked out as he faintly hoped it might, there would be a reward for his friend, and such a reward was worth working for.

He kept telling himself that.

A wolf howled from the hillside, unseen. The doleful sound roused Jim Silver to action. He spoke, and Parade stepped out into a trot, then into a long and sweeping gallop that started him up the wide mouth of the valley, with the hills walking slowly back behind him to either side.

Nothing lived around him, and yet everything seemed at wait, the cactus with its black spot of shadow beside it, the crouching shapes of the hills themselves, and the narrow mouths of the ravines that opened ominously toward him as he went by. It was a moment not easy on the nerves; he wondered how big Dan Farrel was handling the thing.

He thought of Steve Wycombe, too, who had planned his revenge on his enemies so cunningly, as he lay dying. Poison was usually put in food; this was poison placed in rich possessions. Truly Farrel was right, and the soul of Wycombe must be laughing at thought of the evil he had left behind him on earth.

When Silver got up to the head of the valley, where the hills pinched together, he dismounted, let Parade

87

graze on the dusty tufts of grass, here and there, and smoked a cigarette while he walked up and down.

The night was perfectly still now. It seemed as though the slightest sound must necessarily trouble and dim the pure outline of the hills against the moonlight in the sky.

He fell into a mood of absolute quiet. This sort of a time of stillness was, after all, nearer and dearer to him than anything else in life. Neither man nor woman could enter his heart so deeply. So he sat like a stone, only his eyes moving, as he heard Parade crop the grass with slight ripping noises like the tearing of bits of cloth.

He had been there for a long time when, looking up the slope toward the isolated hill of which Farrel had spoken, he saw a red flower bloom in the steep shadow of a rock high above. He knew that it was the signal fire by which Dan Farrel was calling to him for help.

CHAPTER XIV
A RECEPTION COMMITTEE

Dan Farrel, when he trotted his horse away from Silver and up the shallow mouth of the valley that lay between the sprawling hills of the Farrel Mountains and those that descended from Mount Humphreys, felt with every beat of the mustang's right forefoot that he must rein the little horse around and return to tell Silver frankly: "I'm not in this game. I haven't the nerve. I can't do it. The cattle don't belong to me. The land doesn't belong to me. I'm out of the picture."

That would have been talking the way he felt. And finally he swung the mustang sharply around only to find that the lower foothills from the Humphreys range had crawled between him and Silver. He was alone. With the moonlight gleaming in the desert dust, he seemed to be sitting in a thin, ground mist. The hammering of his heart made it hard for him to breathe; it was as though he were submerged in water.

The air was warm enough. He knew that. And yet there was cold inside him. It seemed to come out of the moonlight and run into the marrow of his bones.

"You're a yellow dog," he told himself.

His throat worked on the words. He remembered how he had sat at the table, that night, and how Jim Silver had drawn guns to protect him.

"You're a yellow dog!" he said, out loud.

89

The bigness of his own voice amazed him. He turned his horse around and made it walk up the flat of the valley. As for fellows like Silver, why should they be praised for courage when, as a matter of fact, the God that made them had given them different nerves, different capacities? Does one praise a cat for its skill in catching a bird? No, one simply admires the delicate craftsmanship of nature which can bring foot and eye to such perfection. Does one eulogize the hawk that blows on an easy wing across the heavens?

Then why should Silver be worshiped like a glorious thing when he was simply one of nature's special products, one of her fine elaborations? His eye was surer, his hand was swifter. He could take a fellow like that husky lad, Red, and paralyze him with a grip. At a single gesture he showed himself to be beyond the ken of ordinary people. And as a type of his superiority there was the horse he rode which, to other mustangs, was as an eagle to a crow. From the pursuit of Silver no man in open country could escape. From the pursuit of others, he could easily drift away.

So Farrel kept telling himself over and over again that he was a fool, that he had no business trying to follow the seven-league strides of Jim Silver. And yet, all the while something inside him made him know that he would not give up this fight until bullets or blows had forced him out of it.

He got up to the head of the valley, dismounted, threw the reins off the mustang, and started walking up and down. He was caught, he felt. He was enslaved by an idea, a sense of pride and duty. Was there not a story of the Roman sentinel who kept at his post as the city burned, simply because no orders had come relieving him? And he, Danny Farrel, was like that. He was being a blind and automatic machine. He would get no glory for it, only a hard-nosed bullet out of a Winchester to

90

nudge the life out of him and turn him into food for buzzards.

He looked up the slope of the signal hill, again and again, each time half expecting to see the fire. He was not sure that he would be able to spot the flame. It was perhaps only the dim shimmer of the smoke as it rose through the moonlight that he would be able to distinguish. Or would Silver light the fire in the shadow of a certain tall rock, so that the flames would look out with a redder eye?

He walked up to the top of a low hummock from which he had a better view of the lower valley. He could look out onto the desert itself, which appeared as a thicker streak of mist in the distance.

He came down again to the horse. There was a sudden bond between him and that roach-backed, ewe-necked gelding. He could remember it as a yearling, as a two-year-old. A good set of legs and a body that was like a question mark. Just an ordinary dull-witted, stubborn, headstrong, savage little animal, but now the pressure of fear brought Farrel close to the horse.

The stock of the Winchester that protruded out of the saddle holster was another comfort like the face of a friend. He pulled the gun out, and after handling it a moment, he put it back inside the cover.

If he had had any sense, he would have spent time every day practicing. He would have known that, sooner or later, his life might depend upon his marksmanship. He would have known that it was better to waste a few cartridges for half an hour a day than it was to come to a moment like this. He told himself that therein lay the difference, in part, between himself and men who got on in the world. Fellows like Delgas and Rutherford, for instance, were willing to practice their card tricks and their gun work for hours every free day. That meant that they were prepared when the pinches came, the

91

golden opportunities which so often went hand in hand with terrible dangers.

But as for himself, what was he, and what had he done? He was merely a growth from the soil and attached to it by a blind affection and yearning. He was a thing all root and no tree, like the twisted mesquite. And his labors had been given to riding herd, building fences, doctoring sick cows, tailing them out of mudholes, keeping the night watch, singing to the dogies, breaking mean, down-headed horses, patching sheds. Why, when he died and went over the rim of things into the other world, the ghosts of real men would laugh at him when he tried to describe the still, strange beauty of the desert and the way the three mountains climbed up the northern sky.

He sighed, and then went up to the top of the hummock from which he could look out to the desert. It was just the same with some difference that he could not spot, some small difference.

Then, his mind clearing, he knew what the change was. The sheen of desert dust under the moon was no longer a low, thin streak. It rose much higher, as though a wind were blowing straight up the valley. But something more than the wind might cause the dust to rise.

He looked up at the sky and studied the thin patches of clouds for a moment. No, there was no wind.

So he hurried to his horse, with his heart beating very fast. Still, he must not merely guess, in this fashion. He must not call to Silver with an entirely false alarm.

He threw himself down on the ground and pressed his ear to it. At first he thought that he could hear a distant sound, but finally he knew that it was only the rushing of the blood through the arteries of his head. That noise grew dim, disappeared. Then he could really listen and make out a subdued murmuring. No, it was a rhythm, a pulse, and nothing more. He lay there still, holding his breath, and strained every nerve.

Then he distinguished it clearly—the noise of many, many hoofs trampling.

He was on the back of the mustang in a moment, staring under the shadow of both hands. Now, clearly, he could see the rising of the dust. He thought that he could even make out the twistings of the upper layers of it as the herd entered the mouth of the valley. Perhaps, if the men riding point had sent out a scout well ahead, the puncher in the lead might not be far from him at that moment.

But he gave only a casual glance to the floor of the valley about him. Anger such as he could hardly believe in himself was surging and rising in him. He cast a glance toward the mountains, and marked the jet-black, zigzag traceries of the innumerable canyons against the brightness of the smoother slopes. Once the herd reached that hole-in-the-wall country, pursuit would simply be ridiculous. And therefore, all the early work of his life would be wiped out. It would more than be wiped out. It would be cast into the hands of the two scoundrels, Delgas and Harry Rutherford.

The heat of his anger dissolved all fear. He put the mustang at the slope, and the little horse went up the rough and graveled surface with perfect certainty, straining, throwing itself into its labor as though it perfectly understood.

Right up toward the top they went until they reached that high rock which the glance of Farrel had picked out before this. There was plenty of brush for the kindling of a fire. However, he did not want a great deal. Even the smallest eye of red was likely to meet not only the eye of Silver, in the valley beneath, but also the attention of the men handling the herd, and on a night like this they would be on edge with nervous suspicions.

The brush was tough sage. He tore up some small

93

bushes. The wood resisted his hands when he stripped off the branches. However, he rapidly made a small pile. The leaves which he had shaken off he swept together in a heap, and put a match to them. The flame caught in them. There was a crinkling sound. The red of the fire disappeared. A thickening white smoke went up. The breath of it was pungent and sweet to him. It reminded him of a thousand open camp fires that he had kindled before this, but never had he struck a match that might lead to what would follow now!

The flame burst up through the center of the leaves in a small volcanic eruption of red. He put on little branches of the sage. It burned with a greasy crackling. He put on the larger brush. He stood back and watched the red flower bloom in the shadow of the rock.

He had built it right on the farther edge of this little shoulder, yet it seemed to him that the feeble glow of the flame could not possibly walk so far through the moonlight as to come to the eyes of Jim Silver, in the valley beneath.

He could see that valley. Yes, and now he thought that he could see Silver, far away. A moment later, he was certain. He could not spot man and horse so well, but he was sure of the shadows which they cast on the ground.

Now, as he watched, the man mounted, and began to move straight up the slope toward him. Relief in a warm wave swept through the body and the brain of Dan Farrel. To be alone on such a night was terrible, but to be with such a man as Jim Silver would be exciting, almost glorious, perhaps.

He knew, as he stared down at the climbing form, that he had made no mistake—that he would never regret having ridden out on this night to fight for the herd. Then he thought of Esther and how she had let him go, willingly enough. People like Esther, he felt, always are right. They know how to pick between the easy way and the way of honor and duty and just pride.

After that, he muttered aloud: "Good old Jim Silver."

Something jammed into the small of his back as he stood shaking his head with a new-found affection.

"Yeah," said the voice of Delgas. "He'll be good and old, before very long. Come here, Red. Fan this bird and get his guns. We're goin' to be a reception committee, son. Because that's Jim Silver that's climbin' his horse up the way!"

CHAPTER XV

THE AMBUSH

Farrel was backed up from the edge of the little plateau. If they could see Silver, it was just possible that Silver might be able to spot them. Red stood in front of Farrel and laughed.

"What a simp you are, Danny!" said he. "Why didn't you turn around and look behind you, a couple of times?"

It was strange to Farrel that he felt neither fear nor shame. There had been only a blinding moment of terror when the voice first spoke behind him, but now he could look steadily into the eyes of Red. He had always known the fellow was little good.

"I'm not clever at this sort of work," said Farrel. "I've never spent much time with crooks."

Red had just taken Farrel's Colt. Now he laid the barrel suddenly along the head of Farrel and knocked him staggering.

"Quit that, you fool!" exclaimed Delgas. "We don't want any noise up here. The first thing you know, Silver will hear something. He's got ears like a cat. That's what he is—a cat!"

Delgas was tying the hands of Farrel behind his back. Red, tying a double knot in a big silk bandanna that he folded across, suddenly thrust it between the teeth of Farrel. It made an efficient gag.

"He won't do any yelling to warn Silver. Not just now," said Red.

"Good work," answered Delgas. "You've got a brain, kid. We can use you, maybe—Rutherford and me."

"Jake with me," answered Red. "You know how it is. There ain't any use in punching cows. Ever seen an old cow-puncher? What becomes of 'em, then? They fade away, I tell you."

"They do," agreed Delgas. "The way of it is like this: Those that have got the coin keep it. The poor stiffs that try to work up, they're just playin' into the hands of the millionaire. There's something in the Bible, even, about that. About them that have the goods are going to get the extras, too."

"Yeah, and I've seen it, and I've read it," said Red.

He stepped cautiously across the face of the rock to peer down at the progress of Silver.

"It'll take him a minute," muttered Red. "It's a steep path, and even Parade can't fly that slope. They gotta zigzag up the face of it."

"Sit down," ordered Delgas. "Sit down and rest yourself, kid."

Farrel sat down with his back to the rock.

"What about putting the fire out?" asked Red.

"Sure," agreed Delgas. "That'll make Silver think that Farrel sees him comin'."

Red kicked the fire over the ground. The flames stopped dancing; a broader smudge arose.

The two sat on their heels and waited.

Delgas began to utter his philosophy. "A gent with a bean," he said, "is a gent that knows how to make the easy money. Anybody knows that. And where does the easy money lie? Why, it lies in the other fellow's pocket. And how are you goin' to get it out? By talkin', by turnin' a key, or by usin' a gun. Those are the three ways. There ain't any others. A kid like you, Red, could learn a lot. You could learn to crack a safe, do some confidence steerin', and pack a gun for the pinches."

"Yeah," said Red. "A fellow just has to learn his line. That's all. I guess Rutherford has a line, eh?"

"Thing to listen to," said Delgas, "is that smooth little devil talkin' his way into the confidence of a female. That's where he shines. With a flower in his buttonhole and a hard hat on his head, and with a walkin' stick in his hand and a shine of his shoes, doggone me if it don't do your heart good to see the way he walks right into the heart of a girl. He's slick, is what he is. Understand? He's as slick as they make 'em!"

"Yeah, yeah," muttered Red eagerly. "Wouldn't I like to hear him work, though? Maybe I could do something with the ladies myself. I ain't such a bad hand."

"It's the way he's got of saying the simple things. That's what counts with the females," said Delgas. "You take a woman, they ain't never got more'n the half of a brain in their head. Kind of nutty and foolish. You can't argue with 'em none. You gotta let 'em have their own way or else just sock 'em and let 'em drop. Or else you gotta make love to 'em. That's where Harry shines. He's gotta brain, is what he's got."

"Yeah, he's got a brain," agreed Red, grinning and gaping with admiration.

"Lemme tell you another thing," said Delgas. "A great dodge of Harry's is bein' a recovered consumptive. A lunger that's gone and got well, and he's a millionaire, you see, and he wants to contribute a lot of money to make a big resort where other lungers can go and get well. That's the line he uses in some small town in the Southwest. Anywhere in the Southwest. He gets the whole town all boiled up. He's goin' to build a great big hotel.

98

He's goin' to bring business and lungers on the jump into the place.

"The storekeepers and the ranchers and everybody chips in and raises a nice lot of money. All they gotta do is to deposit as much as the check that Harry puts into the hands of the treasurer of the company, and while Harry's just put in a check, the rest of 'em put in cash. Y'understand? They put in cash and when they've got in the fifteen or twenty thousand dollars which is to show that the town is behind the big idea and willing to help on the street improvements and all of that, then one night the treasurer and Harry disappear, and the town has to sit on its heels and cuss."

Red chuckled softly. "You been the treasurer?" he asked.

"Yeah. I been the treasurer," said Delgas. "Doggone me if I don't laugh till I cry, when I think about some of Harry's stunts. He's gotta brain, is what he's got."

"Look here," said Red. "Whatcha mean by talkin' all these things over in front of Danny?"

"Why," said Delgas, "I got an idea that maybe Danny ain't goin' to live to talk. I got an idea that maybe he'll be lyin' out here mum as a stone, before very long. I just want Harry's O.K. on the job."

Even Red winced a little at this suggestion.

"You're going to—knock him right over the head?" he asked huskily.

"Yeah, and what difference would that make to you? Is he your long-lost brother, or something like that?" asked Delgas, sneering.

"No, no," muttered Red. "Only—well, what Rutherford decides is all right with me."

"He don't go in for the red-handed stuff," agreed Delgas. "Harry is gentle—except when he makes up his mind to be the other thing. What Harry says is that it's a dumb play to go and collect scalps when what you want is wallets. If somebody's gotta be sunk, he'll lay 'em colder'n a stone, all right. But he dodges the trouble. He's that way. He dodges the blood. And I don't blame him. It gets people stirred up when they find blood on the trail. They don't like it. They begin to raise posses. Posses ain't so hard to handle but sometimes they make a little trouble."

"It was a posse that grabbed me and threw me in the can," observed Red thoughtfully.

"You were only a kid and didn't know how to handle yourself," suggested Delgas.

"Yeah. I was only a kid. I hadn't gone to college, at that time. But now that I'm a graduate from the pen, you can bet that I'm wiser. Only, I took a whirl at trying to go straight, till you and Harry come along and showed me that I was making a fool of myself."

"Gents like Rutherford and me, that uses the bean, we don't sit down and take a kick in the face," declared Delgas. "We stand up and kick somebody else."

"Yeah, you do, and you get away with it," said Red, nodding his head.

He began to look with open eyes at Delgas, a sign that his mind was as open as a summer's day, also.

"It's better to kick than to be kicked," said Red.

"Ain't it, though?" agreed Delgas.

"Listen!" said Red.

Over the edge of the hill, Farrel heard the clank of an iron-shod hoof against a stone.

"He's comin' closer," said Delgas. "Listen, kid. This is the greatest chance that you ever had in your life."

"You mean you ain't goin' to take a try at him?" asked Red quickly.

"Sure I'm goin' to take a try at him. We're both goin' to take a try," said Delgas. "But there's enough glory in bumping off Silver to spread thick on two slices, lemme tell you. We're goin' to be known, from now on, as the birds that killed Silvertip. People are goin' to say: 'There goes the birds that bumped off Jim Silver. Those are the ones that killed Arizona Jim.' We're goin' to be pointed out. Understand?"

"Yeah. Sure," said Red. "But he ain't dead yet."

"He's goin' to be dead. Now listen to me. When we sneak up to the edge of the hill, yonder, poke your head over dead easy. Understand? And have your rifle out in front of you. And what you shoot at is the hoss."

"Parade?" said Red. "Morrie, you wouldn't take and kill the finest hoss in the world, would you?"

"Shut up and don't argue," said Delgas, drawing out a pair of Colts from which the sights and triggers had been filed away. "I know best. The job that we got is to bring him down and kill him. And the first stir of anything, that stallion is goin' to jump twenty feet sideways. He's that way. The reason that Silver has got through so many tight holes is mostly that Parade is eyes and ears for him, and a jumpin' fool of a jack-in-the-box, besides. He can smell trouble a mile off down wind, too.

"No, kill that stallion, and Silver is half dead right then. You use your rifle. Make sure. Shoot straight. I'm goin' to use a Colt because I'm sort of more used to it, and if I miss at a cinch of a target like that, call me an old woman and slap my face for me!"

He put down his left-hand gun not far from the feet of Dan Farrel and began to do something to his other Colt.

"It's time!" said Red.

"Wait a minute," commanded Delgas. "Don't rush it. We wanta get there to the ledge just at the right second. I'll tell you when to start. My ears are measurin'

101

the sound and the distance like a tape. I'll tell you when."

He went on: "You gotta learn to fan a gun, kid, and I'm goin' to teach you. It turns loose the bullets like drops of water out of a hose. Now shut up and don't talk. He's too near. And the stallion can hear like a telephone receiver."

So they crouched there, hushed.

Dan Farrel, tied, gagged so that he could hardly breathe, listened to the frantic bumping of his heart. He was wet with sweat. It trickled from his forehead and ran into his helpless eyes. But he saw neither of the men before him clearly; rather he was seeing the big head and shoulders of Silver, swaying a little against the moonlight as Parade carried him lightly up the slope—a perfect target black against the moonlight! One uproar of guns and one thudding of bullets, and that would be the end of him.

It seemed to Farrel like the fall of mountains. He thought of Parade and the death of the great horse was even more impossible than the death of the man. But life can be let out by the prick of a pin. Somewhere he had found that—in a church or in a book.

He wondered if, by a great effort, he could make around the gag some sort of a strangling noise that might be a sufficient warning for Silver. But he knew that he could not manage it. His will was right. He felt that he was willing to die if he could send the message to the man who rode so helplessly into ambush. But he could do nothing.

He twisted in agony, and one foot touched the Colt which had been laid on the ground by Delgas. The electric spark of an idea leaped instantly through his brain. For the hair-trigger weapon was set so that the merest flick of the thumb on the hammer would discharge it,

102

and if he could get his toe on the hammer for an instant—"

Vaguely he saw Red begin to crawl forward, easing the rifle along the ground, moving like a great hunting beast. And over the edge of the hill he distinctly heard the clattering fall of a stone which Parade had dislodged.

The rider was close now. Soon he would be looming above the ledge.

"Now!" whispered Delgas to Red, and reached a hand for the Colt he had put down.

Farrel could not be sure that he would accomplish his purpose. He could only reach out rather blindly and flick back his toe. He felt no resistance more than a mere scratch against the sole of his boot, but a deep explosion boomed instantly in his ear. He had touched the hammer by the grace of chance!

He saw Delgas turn on him like a tiger; he heard the startled snort and plunge of the horse that could not be seen. Then Red had risen to his feet and run forward. On the verge of the ledge, big against the moonlight sky, Red leveled his rifle from the shoulder and fired.

Delgas was instantly beside him, turning loose a stream of bullets.

Both stopped shooting. To look at the dead bodies tumbling down the slope?—wondered Farrel. No, for Delgas was exclaiming:

"Wait—when he comes out from behind the rock— steady—get your bead to the right. I'll watch the left— now—now!"

And again the guns boomed.

Delgas began to spring up and down, cursing. He threw his empty gun on the ground. His yells of rage were like the howling of a beast. But Red, rifle at the ready, was still peering at the distance, trying to get in a final shot.

Farrel took a great breath. Death would be easy to face, he felt, for he had done enough to make his life worthwhile.

Then Delgas turned and rushed snarling back at him.

CHAPTER XVI
THE HERD

Delgas meant murder. The moon was behind his head, but enough of his features showed to let Farrel see the twist and stretch of them, and the catfish gape of his grin. The big fellow took Farrel by the throat. He could not even curse. He could only gasp with the completeness of his rage. With the butt of a revolver he offered to beat Farrel over the head, then to bash in his face.

He could not make a choice when the rifle of Red cracked again and Delgas dropped Farrel flat and ran back to see what had happened.

"I've got him!" yelled Red. "I've got him! Oh, no, he's gone! He's gone. He's made of moonshine, Delgas. Bullets just slide right through him and don't do no harm."

"He'll moonshine you when he lays his hands on you!" said Morris Delgas. "He'll show you what moonshine can do, you flathead! What you got a rifle for? What you good for, you four-flusher, you fake of a wooden Injun?"

Red gradually straightened under the pouring of the abuse. At last he said: "That's about enough out of your trap, Delgas."

"It's enough, is it?" shouted Delgas. "I'll show you what's enough! I'm goin' to see what's inside you! I'm goin' to take a look at your lining!"

He put his great grasp on Red, who slid one hand

behind him as if to get at a knife. For a moment, they faced each other. Then Delgas cursed and took his hands away from Red.

"I oughta eat your heart," he vowed, "but it'd be that much the better for the skunk that's lyin' yonder laughin' at us! It'd be fine for him if we choked each other and rolled down the slope here and bashed our heads in. Wouldn't that be slick for him?"

"I done the best shootin' I could," said Red. "But that hoss was maneuverin' all the time like a snipe flyin' down wind. There wasn't no regularity about nothin' he did. He didn't keep to no straight lines, the fool. You seen that for yourself, Delgas. You had a pretty close shot at him, but you couldn't hit him."

"It was Farrel that give him a couple of winks of head start," argued Delgas. "The shootin' off of the gun was what started that hawk flyin', and two flaps takes a bird like that a long ways. Red, I'm sorry I started in to manhandle you. It wasn't your fault. But for a second, all I could think of was that Jim Silver had been inside our hands—and that we let him slip!"

"I know," said Red. "I know how you feel. Don't I feel the same way, though? It's hell, is all that it is!"

They went back to Farrel and stood over him. The hands of Morris Delgas worked at his sides. They looked to Farrel like the jaws of two fish biting at the air. He kicked Farrel in the ribs.

"Get up!" he commanded.

The pain of the bruised flesh sickened Farrel. The weight of the blow made it difficult for him to breathe, but he got slowly to his feet. He realized that the least hesitation might hasten his time of dying.

So he stood and confronted the pair of them. And suddenly, Delgas reached out and removed the bandanna that gagged Farrel.

"You done the noble thing, didn't you?" asked Delgas. "Hey? It was noble, wasn't it?"

Farrel said nothing.

"Answer me!" shouted Delgas. "You was being noble, wasn't you?"

Farrel said nothing. He saw Delgas swing back a fist and how the punch traveled right at his head. He had an idea that he might be able to duck the blow, but if he avoided it, he was reasonably sure that he would be murdered. It was what Delgas wanted—the least additional excuse so that he would not be killing a helpless man in cold blood. So Farrel stood still and let the fist strike him in the face.

Once he had been struck down when the massive shoulder of a hay wagon nudged him. The fist of Delgas was like that. It seemed to be faced with brass and to have a ton of driving weight behind it. It took him right off his feet and slammed him down on the back of his head. He could hear the whack of the fist against his flesh as though two hands had been clapped together. Afterward, he heard his head pound solidly against the rock.

When his wits cleared, a second later, the left side of his face was numb, with liquid trickling over the skin, tickling it. Then he realized that his cheek bone had been laid open and the blood was running down from that.

Big Morris Delgas got him by the hair of his head and jerked him to a sitting posture. He swung back his other fist.

"I asked you, was you being noble?" shouted Delgas. "I asked you was you a dirty hound that was being noble, shooting a gun by a kick of your foot, giving Jim Silver warning. I asked you was you a dirty rat, a dirty noble rat? Was you?"

107

He kept jerking the head of Farrel back and forth, and his right hand oscillated with terrible eagerness to beat again into the face of the prisoner.

Red broke in suddenly: "Aw, back up, Delgas. Let him be."

Delgas dropped Dan Farrel and whirled about.

"You want something?" he yelled.

Red had backed up a little. He had his hand behind him again, and Farrel could see how the fingers were looped over the handle of a knife. He seemed to mean business, though he kept on backing up, slowly, before the truculent advance of Delgas.

"I won't take water from you, Delgas," he said.

"You're butting in, you fool!" shouted Delgas, wavering with the wind of his fury. "You're butting in and you're tryin' to tell me what's what. I'm goin' to smash you!"

Red kept on backing up, more and more slowly.

"I won't take water from nobody," he said.

He stood still, suddenly.

"I won't take water from you, Delgas," he said.

His hand came around from the small of his back. The moonlight winked along the blade of the sharpened steel.

Delgas strode close and measured himself against Red. He was so big that he had only to throw out his arms in order to embrace the smaller man. The whole body of Delgas worked in his passion, just as the entire body of a vast cat might work, as it sharpens its claws.

"You poor fool," said Delgas, "d'you think your toad sticker can stop me?"

"I don't think nothing," said Red. "I just think that I won't take water from nobody."

"I got a mind to bash your head in," said Delgas.

"All right. I guess you're big enough to bash me," said

Red, "but you gotta prove it. I ain't taking water from nobody."

"What's the matter with you, kid?" demanded Delgas. "Are you nutty or something? What you butting in for?"

"I don't care about him," said Red. "You can take and drill him through the head, for all I care, or open him up with a knife, and it's Jake with me. But I hate you to be beating up a bird that can't lift his hands."

"What's the matter with you? You ain't takin' the socks, are you?" asked Delgas.

"I dunno. It sort of makes me sick," said Red.

Delgas laughed. "You are funny," he said. "That is what you are. You're just a funny hombre. I bang him in the mug and you take and get sick. You're just a funny hombre, is what you are, Red."

"All right," said Red. "I can't help it."

"Sure you can't help it, if you're built that way," said Delgas. "Besides, I dunno that it's a good idea to smear up this gent too much. Maybe it's better to wait till Harry Rutherford has a look at him. Harry might have some ideas about the way to handle him, I guess."

"Sure he might," agreed Red. "Now you're talking, old son. We'll get him back to Rutherford, down yonder, and see what Harry has to say about him."

Delgas nodded. He concluded the argument on which the life of Farrel had depended by saying: "He thought he was being noble, was what made me sore. Reaching out and shooting the gun to warn his friend—you know, kind of being noble and giving himself away to the Injuns for the sake of his partner—you know, regular story stuff. That was what made me sick, him playing noble, like that. That's why I asked him was he trying to be noble. If he'd said yes, I would 'a' bashed him to a pulp!"

They mounted Farrel on his horse, tying its lead rope to the pommel of Delgas's saddle, after the other two

109

climbed on their own horses, which had been left a little down the slope. And Farrel found himself looking down to a great wave of turmoil that swept up through the valley gradually.

Over it, a great billowing mist came up in waves. There seemed to be no wind, and yet the dust kept on rising. The acrid taint of it began to stain the air around Farrel. He could look down into the thin fog and see through it the swaying, pouring multitudes of the herd. Right across the valley they spread.

They moved as a front of water moves. Sometimes a pressure of some sort caused one section to roll swiftly out ahead of the rest of the front, and then that section was delayed, as though the dry sands were drinking up the current, and another portion of the front lurched into the lead. Waves like those of water passed through the herd, also; vague perturbations and disturbances of the living mass. And the clatter and rattle of the clashing hoofs and the striking horns beat up to Farrel like a vast cymbal chorus, while the calves bawled high and the bulls roared low.

And he was the maker of that great herd. He could remember the day when he talked to old Wycombe, that cunning fox who had been the father of the dead man. He had said: "Mr. Wycombe, I'm fifteen. That's why I'm willing to start small and work big. You wait and see. I know the right sort of a steer to run on this sort of land. I can breed 'em, and I can buy 'em, too. I know beef as I know the flat of my own hand."

Old Wycombe had listened, and smiled, and listened. That was the day Farrel began to be a slave to an idea, and to the Wycombe family, and finally he had built up his herd, in actual fact. The size of it seemed to be magnified by the moonlight. It was flooding through his heart and soul. The mountains seemed to be trembling with the thunder of the multitude. He kept on saying to himself soundlessly: "I did all of that. I raised that herd. And now it's going to be wasted. Now it's going to be wasted."

Big Delgas, reining close to him, said: "Your face is all swelling up, kid. I'm sorry that I socked you like that. But you made me sore. It makes me sore to see a gent trying to be noble. It makes me mad, is all it does."

Farrel shrugged his shoulders.

"He's thinking about the beef. He's not thinking about himself," remarked Red, with a touch of both curiosity and of sympathy in his voice.

"What you mean, he's thinking about the beef?" said Delgas.

"Down there," said Red, gesturing. "He's not so sorry for the beating he got, but he's sorry to see his herd break up."

"He never owned no part of it," answered Degas.

"He built it, brother, is what I mean," said Red. "You gotta understand how you'd feel if you'd built something and seen it go smash."

"Like a toy house. I know," said Delgas. "My big brother built a kind of a toy house, one day. I come along and took and give it a shove, and it goes in a pile. Was he sore? He was sore, lemme tell you. He up and after me. And I went high-tailin' through the house and outside, and he took and made a high dive off the back porch and caught me, and then did he pretty near kill me? I'll tell a man he done just that. He was kind of sore because I'd spilled his house. But this guy is funny, that wants to cry when he sees his herd break up—his herd that he don't own no hair of."

Suddenly Farrel found himself, quite outside of his own expectations, making an explanation.

"Suppose you had a big stretch of land," he said. "Suppose you have a big stock of water behind a dam. Feed it out slow, and you've got water for the whole year through. Bust the dam, and it's all gone in a day, and the ranch is thrown away. That's the way I feel. Those cows are going to spill away through the hills and split up into a hundred different sections. Who's buying them? Sam Waring?"

The heads of both Red and Delgas jerked suddenly.

"Never mind who's buying them," said Delgas. "Worry about the coin that's comin' into your own pocket, not what's comin' into mine!"

CHAPTER XVII
SAM WARING

They talked for a moment as to which end of the herd they should aim at—the rear of it or the point. Because the cattle were not being pushed ahead into the mountains. There was no very great hurry, for that matter, and, since the herding by daylight would be more assured work than herding them by night, perhaps the herd would be kept here until close to daylight, which was not very far off in any event.

Finally it was decided to go down the slope to the point of the herd, where it was held by several riders at the head of the valley. They descended rapidly, and, coming out into the open, they were assailed by angry cries that ordered them to get to work. The punchers were working short-handed, in trying to hold that confused mob of steers. But one puncher, coming near enough to identify faces, raised a whoop of exctied triumph at the sight of Farrel. He went off, waving his hat in circles and yelling like a wolf.

"Your punchers don't seem to think much of you, kid," said Delgas, laughing.

Farrel made no answer. Now that he was at close range, even through the rolling and thick, fog-white outpouring of the dust, he could recognize steer and cow and calf that he had handled himself. And he ran his eyes with a strange love over the long shanks of the cattle, and the straight, lean bellies, and the high, lean backs. No sign of roaching in those backs, and no sign of weakness in the quarters. They were built like deer. They could move to forage. They could run a whole day for water after they had lived on dry feed for two days.

That line of cattle was not his discovery. The Spanish had bred it in a small version centuries before; the Texans had bred it big in more recent times; but he knew the particular brand and type that suited this special bit of desert range. He knew it like a book, and he had made it. Now it was to go. It was to pour away through the mountain canyons and be dissipated like water running through a sieve. He turned his head away. He could not face the wretched thought of all that wasted labor.

He knew now, suddenly, that a man lives not for the sake of putting hard cash into his own pocket, but for the sake of some sort of creation—a store, a poem, a herd of cows. It was all the same. To build up something where there was nothing before—that was the feeling that drove decent men. And now, in stealing the herd, they were stealing a portion of his life that could never be returned to him. The dollars could go to the devil. But time is more priceless, and it was time which they would be wasting.

Delgas aimed for a flicker of firelight that was visible at the very point of the valley, where the foot of a hill was splintered into a great shagginess of rocks. When they drew closer to the firelight, a man stood up, and they saw the sheen of the long barrel of a rifle.

This fellow, who seemed to be a guard, sang out:

"Yeah? Yeah? Which way, waddies?"

"Delgas speakin'!" called Delgas.

"That don't mean nothin' to me," said the other.

"One of the others," said Red. He added loudly: "Is Rutherford around?"

"Rutherford is here," said the puncher with the rifle.

"If that means much to you, he's here and he's busy."

"Take this hombre," said Delgas.

He dismounted, threw the reins of his horse to Red, and walked ahead. After a few words with the guard, he called for the others to come, and Red led in Farrel to the verge of the rocks.

The fire was blazing merrily behind them. A pair of unshaven fellows had drawn off portions of the main blaze, and on these smaller fires they were frying bacon and bringing coffee to a boil. The scent of the food was good in the nostrils of Farrel. He told himself that he would remember this—that even in the midst of misery he was able to feel hunger and desire food as though he had simply come to the end of a long, hard, successful day's work.

Tethered close by, here and there, stood several good-looking horses, and a mule whose pack was being unloaded.

"Go easy with that pack, you fool!" sang out a voice. "There's dynamite in that!"

Everyone raised a shout at the word.

Rutherford alone did not stir. He was sitting cross-legged in front of a flat slab of rock, counting out stacks of greenbacks and weighing them down, one after another, with stones. Beside him stood the big, rounded paunch and the fat face of Sam Waring, crook extraordinary.

After the confusion caused by the word about dynamite had died down, Delgas came close up and leaned over Rutherford.

"We've got Danny Farrel," he said. "We nearly got Silver, too."

"You nearly got hell," said Rutherford, without looking up, continuing his count.

"Farrel was signaling him," said Delgas. "We waited, and Silver came right up the hill, but Farrel managed

115

to kick the hammer of my gun, and the shot scared Silver away like a wild duck."

"You talking about Arizona Jim? You talking about Jim Silver?" demanded Waring, shifting the butt of his cigar rapidly across his wide mouth.

"That's the hombre," said Delgas.

"I don't want any part of him!" said Sam Waring hastily.

He threw out both hands in a great gesture to emphasize his point.

"I don't want any part in him at all!" he shouted.

"I told you he was on deck," said Rutherford.

"You told me you'd have him under cover," answered Waring.

"The fool ought to be," said Rutherford. "We left him under cover, and he should have stayed there; but—well, I've felt in my bones that I'd have it out with him, before long."

"Have it out with him by yourself," remarked Waring. "I don't want any part of him. He's 'Mr. Silver,' and 'your honor,' and anything he wants, so far as I'm concerned."

"Oh, shut up, Waring," said Rutherford. "You're not going to pull out because of Jim Silver."

"If I'd known he was to be on the loose," said Waring, "I'd never 'a' worked into this here deal. I'm a peaceable man. I don't want any hell for pepper in my soup, thanks. I'm no fightin' man, Rutherford, and you know it."

"You've got plenty of thugs along to do your fighting for you," said Rutherford.

"I'm an old man," answered Waring, who looked about fifty by the gray of his hair and the lines in his face. "But there's still a mite of life in me, and I don't want to drain it out. One small bullet hole will let a million dollars' worth run out and go to waste in half a second, brother. And I know it."

Something else took the attention of Waring, a moment later, and, before any one could comment on his last speech, he pointed silently at Farrel.

"That! Who brought that man in here?" said Waring.

"What's the matter with him?" asked Delgas.

"He's not in on the deal!" exclaimed Waring. "What are you fellows trying to do? Advertise me in the newspapers?"

He was very excited, and began to beat a fist into the fat palm of his hand.

"Keep your hat on," advised Delgas. "He ain't goin' to do you no harm."

"What's the matter, Sam?" asked Farrel.

"It's Danny Farrel," said Waring, "and he knows me as well as I'd know my own father. You fellows are crazy loons! Why'd you bring him in here, anyway?"

Rutherford looked up from his counting.

"Maybe he knows too much, anyway, before he saw you. If he knows too much, maybe we'll have to make him forget it, Sam."

"What you mean?" asked Waring.

Rutherford slid a forefinger, slowly, across his scrawny neck.

"Oh," groaned Waring, "do we have to have that kind of dirty work?"

"Yeah?" said Delgas. "It's *your* laundry that we're worryin' about, Sam."

Waring snapped his fat fingers high above his head. He was very impatient.

"It's a bad business," he said.

"Worse for Farrel than for you," added Delgas.

Waring turned his back and began to walk up and down, puffing rapidly at his cigar until a veil of white formed about his head, and he kept striding back and forth through it, making gestures of protest and annoyance.

117

Rutherford continued his counting, laying small stones on the heaps that he put out on the rock.

"That's a lot of kale you been carrying around with you, Waring," observed Delgas.

"Cash is better than carry," said Waring shortly.

He stopped in his pacing and pointed at Farrel.

"Something's gotta be done," he said.

"Do it yourself, then. I guess that nobody would stop you," said Delgas. "I don't love him none. My knuckles are what cut him up, the poor sucker."

"Come out with it," urged Rutherford. "You want him bumped off now, Waring?"

"Wait a minute," said Waring. "Let's think it over. Maybe something can be done with him."

The heart of Farrel, which had turned to ice, began to beat again.

"Get that canvas sack away from the fire!" suddenly shouted some one. "That's the dynamite, you fools!"

The man who was carrying the tarpaulin almost dropped it, and when he had lowered it to the ground, he jumped a rod.

"Why didn't you say so before?" he yelled. "I got a good mind—"

"You got a good mind to back up, and that's what you're goin' to do," said an unshaven brute, swaying to his feet from beside the fire.

Waring turned and raised one hand.

"Stop!" he commenced. "Brick, take that dynamite back from the fire."

"Brick," who had just risen ready for fight, snarled under his breath, but he picked up the tarpaulin and carried it to a crevice between two of the rocks.

"The point is," said Waring, "that we've got this fellow Farrel on our hands, and Jim Silver ready to poison us somewhere in the open, loose and freehanded! Silver's

118

enough to have on the mind. And you have to tell me if Farrel can be handled."

"He can't be handled," said Rutherford, still counting. "He's one of the fools who prefer to be honest if they have to die for it."

"He's the kind of a fool," broke in Delgas, "that wants to do something noble. That's the kind that he is."

And Farrel knew that he was listening to his death sentence.

CHAPTER XVIII

A COOL BIRD

One man more than those who could be counted around the fire had heard the last speech. That was Jim Silver, who had fled from the warning sound of the shot as he rode toward the signal smoke, and who had rounded through the upper shoulder of Mount Humphreys and come down again toward the face of the herd that was now in full view, sweeping into the valley.

Farrel was gone, that was clear. His own single pair of hands could probably do nothing; but, nevertheless, he did not turn back or ride for help in the town. He kept on toward the perils of one more "last chance."

A long, sharp-sided ravine gave him a good slant toward the head of the valley. When he came out of that ravine, he was low down the slope and he could see the fluttering of the firelight among rocks at the base of the hill.

Therefore, he left the great stallion behind him and came on foot, worming his way here and there, never knowing when the upthrust of a hand of fire might show him to hostile eyes. And sometimes it seemed to Silver, as he came in closer, that the light was focused upon him out of a lantern, and that eyes were fixed upon him. It seemed as though voices were raised in laughing mockery while he drew nearer. Guns must be watching him. Fingers must be curling contentedly around the polished curve of triggers.

But he came on up until the blackness of the shadows at close hand shielded him from the light of the fire, and there was only the moon to consider. That was comparatively simple, because the shadow of the next hill now sloped across half of the rock nest inside of which the fire was burning. That was why Silver was able to draw so very close up to the point of danger and of interest.

He had arrived in time to see and hear all that had recently passed. He had had the uncomfortable experience of seeing the sack of dynamite placed right before the spot where he cowered. He used it, afterward, as a better cover which enabled him to draw nearer.

So he heard the death sentence passed on Farrel, in simple words.

"Look, Farrel," said Sam Waring, striding suddenly up to the prisoner. "Don't you go and be a fool. You come along with us. I'll take care of you. You come along with me. I'll give you a regular split in the job. I'll take care of you. I don't want the blood of any kid on my hands."

"It ain't any good," argued Delgas. "There we had him tied and gagged and stretched all out, and the fool, he wants to be noble and kicks my gun and makes it go off and scare away that bird, Silver. A gent that wants to be noble," said Delgas, "ain't any use to birds like us. You know that, Sam."

"Shut up, Morrie," said Waring. "I know plenty. I'm asking the kid. It's up to you, Danny. Will you play with us?"

Silver risked being seen, as he lifted his head to stare into the face of Farrell. That face was puffed and blood-streaked. It was set, too, in hard lines of endurance. The

121

eyes glistened as Farrel stared back at Waring.

"We've all gotta die once," said Farrel.

"Oh, hell!" said Waring, turning on his heel.

He threw up his hands, as though to ask the world's attention to the effort that he had been willing to make on behalf of this young fool.

"I told you," said Delgas.

"Yeah, you told me," said Waring. "I wouldn't believe anybody'd be such a fool. Look here, Danny!"

He whirled and faced Farrel again.

"Everybody's laughing at you, you half-wit," said he. "Don't hold out on us, Danny. Come in and play the game, will you? What's the matter with you?"

"He's nuts about a girl that cooks back there on the ranch," said Delgas. "Look at, kid," said Delgas, stepping suddenly close to Farrel. "She don't care about you. She was only givin' you a play, that's all. She'd pick up anybody. She give me the sweet eye, is what she done. She's just stringing you along."

"You lie!" said Farrel.

"You see?" said Delgas, stepping back and turning his hands palms up. "He's goin' to be noble, that's all. He's nuts about the girl, and he's goin' to be noble. She'll be married to some other sap about a week after the coyotes finish lickin' his bones, but he's goin' to die noble and believe in her to the finish."

"Shut up, Morrie," commanded Waring again. "Let me talk to him. Listen to me, kid, will you?"

Farrel looked straight a Waring and said nothing.

"I'm giving you a break," said Waring. "Wake up to it, hombre. I'm giving you a break, and you don't know it. Will you take a hand in our game?"

"Thanks," said Farrel.

"Thanks what? Yes, or no?"

"Thanks—no," said Farrel.

The hair prickled on the head of Jim Silver, as he

heard that. He took out both revolvers and made his calculations. There was plenty of cover all around. He might get two or three of them before the rest were out of sight. He might even let Farrel have a chance to get to him. But after that?

Well, after that, they'd be done for. Nothing could save them—not when fellows like Delgas and Waring and Rutherford were around. For all the pretended strength of his hatred for blood, Waring was the sort of a marksman who cannot miss, and Silver knew it very well.

It was not of Rutherford's pale face that Silver thought most, now. It was of the bucktoothed smile of Steve Wycombe, his upper lips caught and hanging. That was the way he must be smiling now. For it began to look a good bet that all the men he wanted to get would go down—Rutherford, Delgas, and Jim Silver, all three.

Decent men, it seemed to Silver, have fewer brains than rascals. Otherwise, such an inspiration could never have come into the head of Steve Wycombe.

"You won't play with us?" repeated Waring.

"He won't," said Delgas. "He's scared stiff, and he's dyin' on his feet with fear; but he's gotta be noble, the sucker! Give him the works and get rid of him, will you?"

"You talk as if you'd like the job," Waring said. "Take it, Delgas. I give you my share in him."

"Am I goin' to stick pigs for you, Sam?" demanded Delgas. "Since when, I'd like to know!"

"All right," said Waring. "It'll have to be fixed some way. One of my boys will turn the trick, I suppose. Too bad, though, because he's a pretty good kid."

"Sam," said the voice of Rutherford.

"Keep your eye on Farrel," said Waring to the man called "Brick." "He needs plenty of watching. One fellow

123

like that, loose in the world, could spoil my future for me."

"Your future's like a fish a week out of water," said Brick gloomily, but he took up his post beside Farrel.

"What is it, Harry?" Waring was asking, while Silver breathed more easily for the moment.

He began to cudgel his brains. He had a conviction that, no matter how tight the pinch, no matter how hopeless a situation might be, there was always some way of solving it, some way of cutting the Gordian knot. Now he felt fairly baffled, but baffled he must not be.

He began to strain his wits. Then he told himself that ideas would not come in that fashion. Instead, he must lie still, passively, and wait for whatever would come to him. So, little by little, he relaxed.

There was a promise that he might gain a little time, for Rutherford and Waring were wrangling hotly.

"Sorry, Sam," Rutherford said. "Looks as though you're just fifty-seven hundred dollars short in the payment."

"Hey!" shouted Waring, starting violently.

Rutherford was not in the least moved. He lifted his pale face and studied Waring with a calm interest.

"What you mean by fifty-seven hundred short?" demanded Waring.

"I mean five thousand and seven hundred dollars and no cents," said Rutherford. "I mean that money's short."

"It was in the pile when I handed it to you," declared Waring.

Very gradually a smile spread over the features of Rutherford. He shook his head.

"It was in the satchel when I handed it to you," said Waring.

Rutherford kept on smiling.

"What the devil's the matter, Harry?" asked Waring

"You don't think that I'd try to cheat you, do you?"

"You know, brother," said Rutherford, "that we all look for a little inside profit. You wouldn't call it stealing."

"Why, Harry," said Waring, "I'm kind of shocked by this here. It couldn't be that Ferris would 'a' hooked a handful of dough out of that satchel, could it? You don't really mean that the coin's missing, though? You're just laughin' up your sleeve at me."

Rutherford continued to smile.

"When you get through talking, Sam," said he, "just grab the extra cash and hand it over."

"You don't understand," said Waring. "Where would I get that much loose cash out of a crowd like this? Every bean that I've got is right in there. But I'll see you in a couple or three days."

"I won't be around," said Harry Rutherford. "But don't you worry about the extra money, Sam."

"No? Thanks," said Waring. "I knew you wouldn't try to hang up a deal like this on account of a measly little five or six thousand. I'll fix it with you, one day, as straight as a road."

"Of course you will," said the quiet voice of Rutherford. "You'll fix it now. I'll just take that big rock you wear in your necktie, brother."

"I'm not wearing that diamond now, Harry," said Waring.

"Not at your neck in the bandanna," agreed Rutherford. "You have it pinned under the lapel of your coat."

"What?" exclaimed Sam Waring. "How did you—"

He broke off his protesting argument and shouted with laughter.

"Hey, but you're a cool bird, Harry," he said. "Did anybody ever put anything over on you?"

"Not one, except Steve Wycombe, and he's wearing

125

the scars of the good turn he did for me. Let's see the hard cash, brother."

"Sure," said Waring.

And the brazen cheat instantly pulled out a wallet and counted the extra cash into the hand of Rutherford.

CHAPTER XIX
STAMPEDE

By this time, clouds of dust raised by the milling cattle were pouring in rapid drifts across the camp fire, turning into grit the food which the men were eating, scumming across the surface of the coffee. All complexions became gray in a moment. It was a fog, and not a thin fog, that surrounded the fire and that made the moon dim.

Silver, with the razor edge of a knife, slit the tarpaulin that covered the dynamite. Inside was a quantity of sawdust; inside the sawdust lay the corded sticks of the explosive, each one carefully wrapped. He took out half a dozen of them, short lengths, and found a quantity of fuse, also. That was what he wanted. He hardly dared to look at Dan Farrel, in the meantime, for the moment of Dan's death was close at hand, plainly.

He heard Red make a feeble protest.

"This here is a fellow that would keep his mouth shut," said Red. "You could trust him, Waring. If he said he wouldn't talk about you, he'd keep his word."

Waring went up to Red and laid a fatherly hand on his shoulder.

"My dear young feller," said Waring. "You're just in the make and you ain't finished, yet, or else I'd be bothered about you. I'd say that maybe you had a lot to learn about the way folks act when they're under temptation.

Now, you take young Farrel here. I'd say that he's a fine lad and an honest lad and a lad that means well, but I wouldn't be able to tell what he might do after givin' us his word here. He might be tempted—"

Here Farrel broke in, his voice dry and harsh: "If I ever had a chance to hang the whole crew of you, I'd do it. I'd give my life to do it."

The words fell like a blow on Jim Silver. He barely heard the voice of Waring continuing: "There! You can see for yourself what things are like. You can see for yourself that he ain't the sort of a fellow that would make a nice, reasonable bargain, is he?"

"I dunno," said Red. "I'm kind of sick, is all I know."

That was the last that Silver heard as he withdrew like a snake among the rocks. The sweeping of the dust from the herd covered him, and the thickness of the uproar of clashing hoofs and horns, the pounding, the bellowing seemed to conceal him under a blanket of noise. The sound of a cataract draws down all eyes into it, and in the same manner, perhaps, all looks would be centering now upon the milling of the herd.

So he took chances of being seen as he hurried back toward the stallion. At any moment, even in a few seconds after he turned his back on the camp-fire scene, the thrust of a knife or the explosion of a gun might be the end of Farrel.

If Farrel died, he swore that he would spend the rest of his days tracking down every man who had appeared around that fire. But all that quantity of revenge would not bring back life to Danny Farrel or ease the heart of the girl who had sent him away to do his duty on this night.

So Silver worked with frantic haste, as he kneeled beside Parade, at last, attaching to each of the dynamite sticks a fuse of the length he had decided upon. He had three sticks and three fuses, each a little longer than the other, when he finally mounted. He proposed to save Farrel, if he could, not by shooting down the men who stood around him—there were too many of these—but by sweeping the whole gang away in the current of an action that promised to carry out from their hands the entire profits of the adventure on which they had embarked.

So he rode Parade right down the gulley to the point where it shelved off to meet the valley floor and the sweeping dust clouds which drove up above the herd and circled in the light wind toward the moon. He was doubly glad of that screen of dust now.

Closely as he harkened, he had not distinguished the sound of a gun during the interim. Perhaps Rutherford and Delgas and Waring were patching up the last details of their agreement; perhaps they intended to wait until the final moment before the herd was pushed up into the hills before they killed Dan Farrel and left him on the ground to be battered by the trampling hoofs beyond all recognition.

Silver scratched a match.

"Hey, Ferris, is that you?" yelled a voice not far away. "Cut in there and do your bit! Climb into it, kid!"

Silver touched the flame of the match to the ends of the three fuses, one quite short, the others longer. He had three portions of death in his grasp then. Even Parade, steel-nerved under most circumstances, now began to dance uneasily as he saw the sparkling blue fire run sputtering up the fuses.

Silver, with a yell, drove the stallion straight at the herd.

Off to his right, he saw a rider phantom-gray in the dust, and heard the man cursing with bewildered surprise. The sweep of the outer flank of the milling cattle came into clearer view. He saw the dull sheen of their eyes, the tossing of the horns like crooked spears continually stabbing at the air, and full at the mass of them he threw the dynamite with the shortest fuse attached.

It had seemed to him that he had waited until the fire was fairly kissing the dynamite, and yet there was no uproar of an explosion. Instead, the dynamite rolled under the feet of the first steers and was instantly out of sight.

He turned the stallion, with a groan, to try again farther down the head of the crowding cattle. Then, behind him, he heard the explosion and felt the weight of it in the air about him, a soft and ponderous blow that made Parade leap like a hare.

Glancing back, he could see several of the steers down, struggling. Those poor, mangled creatures would never rise again. But from about them the rest of the cattle were pressing back, throwing up their heads, trying to climb over the backs of the steers which still were surging up from the depths of the valley. It seemed to Silver that he had done no more than throw a bucket of water against the sweep of a sea, so small was the reaction.

But he went on, yelling like a fiend.

The second fuse had burned short. He set his teeth, counted three, and flung it. It burst in the very air, flattening several animals. He went on and cast the third stick far over against the farther side of the valley's head, into the thick of the steers.

Again some of the poor creatures went down. But the rest were turning rapidly to escape these thunderbolts. With a frantic bawling the entire front of the herd wheeled and pressed back. It was slow work. The mass of the cattle remained before the terrified vanguard, a living wall against retreat unless the panic should spread to them.

Right and left, now, Silver saw riders making toward him. He heard the shouting of the many voices. He thought he could make out the tremendous uproar of

Delgas above the rest, thundering like a wounded bull.

For his own part, Silver was pushing close in behind the van, close into the stifling fog of dust through which he was only vaguely aware of the twisting, swirling masses of confused backs, and of swaying horns. It made him dizzy, like looking into the fling and leap of water as it runs down a cataract.

He shouted; he yelled; he fired guns in the face of any beast that chanced to turn back toward him. Far before him, he could hear the rear guard of cow-punchers shooting their Colts to keep the cattle near them from turning in a stampede.

Close beside him, a voice drove in, screaming out curses. A bullet touched his hat, jerked at it with a small but deadly touch. He shot that fellow out of the saddle and saw the frightened cow pony go crash into the wall of the herd.

But it was no longer quite a solid wall. It was splitting up. A shudder was working through the mass of the steers; the solidity of the throng opened into cracks that filled, closed, opened again. It was like watching a quick-sand at work. Then all that quicksand began to flow, slowly, more quickly, as fast as a man could run, as fast, almost, as a horse could gallop.

Parade followed close to the swinging tails.

It was dangerous work. The dust streamed back at them in dense up-pourings that blinded the eyes. But eyes were needed to see the crumpled, red-washed bodies that lay on ground, here and there, where some unlucky steer had fallen and been beaten instantly to death by heavy hoofs.

Through rifts in the flying dust, Silver, muffled to the eyes in a bandanna so that breathing could be possible, saw the walls of the ravine, one black with shadow, one gleaming with the moon.

That gleaming wall he saw thrust out a straight-faced

131

bluff where the valley narrowed a trifle. It was easy to see and easy to avoid, with the moon striking the front of it as if it glanced from white marble; but the steers could not turn, no matter what they saw through the blindness of their fear. There was no shifting inward, because the little valley was blocked from side to side, jammed with the sweep of the running cattle. There was no halting or turning back, because the rearward cattle picked up those in front and hurled them forward.

So Silver saw a living wave strike the face of that bluff, pile instantly high on it, bank the angle full with the dead, and so shunt the remnant safely past the danger point.

It was enough to break a man's heart to see good beef wasted in this fashion, but in a moment like that the salvation of the entire herd was what Silver had to think of.

Then, before him, he saw the herd thinning. He knew by that that they were approaching the mouth of the valley. Presently the dust cloud thinned away. Breaths and puffs of sweet, fresh air came to him like a salvation. The myriad beating of the hoofs no more kept the ground quivering beneath him, but scattered far and wide.

He rode off to the right, drawing up Parade to a canter. He was off to the side of the valley's mouth when he saw other riders fly by him, half revealed through the dust, sweeping on to head off the stampede, if possible.

But Silver, drawing back into a corner of the hills, observed the onward course of the living avalanche which he had started and was content. Stampeding steers are not easily turned, and they do not easily lose their momentum. Far, far away across the desert the dust cloud blew, rolled small and smaller, dwindled, seemed no more than an obscure smoke that was barely visible beneath the moon.

After it had dwindled like this, he saw, from his shadow-filled cranny, the thing that he had hoped to see.

Out of the valley's mouth proceeded a small group of riders, among whom he recognized Rutherford, Waring, and Red. With them came a tall fellow who sat with his hands tied behind his back and had his horse's lead rope attached to Waring's saddle.

That was poor Danny Farrel. The stampede had given him the grace of a little more life, but in a way it seemed to have made his death almost the more sure. For every one of the group would be savagely hungry for blood after the disappointment of that night.

CHAPTER XX
WARING'S PROPOSITION

Moonlight swallows things quickly, even when there is the clear air of the desert for it to shine through. That cavalcade disappeared and left an ache in the back of Silver's brain as he recalled the straight back and the high head of poor Dan Farrel.

Why had they saved him? Perhaps—it had been Silver's hope from the first—because with the cattle scattered and Jim Silver abroad to make further mischief, Rutherford and the rest would be glad to have him alive as a bargaining point.

It was in this hope that he calmly unsaddled Parade that night, wrapped himself in slicker and blanket, and, with the saddle for a pillow went to sleep.

Twice Parade wakened him, snuffing close to his face and stamping to give the alarm. Once it was merely a wolf that had come out on the shoulder of the hill to look down on man. Once it was for some taint that had blown to Parade on the air; but, when Silver could see nothing, he lay down again and slept peacefully until the sun put a warm hand on his face.

He got up, washed his eyes and mouth with water from his canteen, swallowed a few drops of the liquid, and then pulled up his belt two notches to take the place of breakfast. Parade, grazing the tough gramma grass at a short distance from his master, came back and stood with downward head, dozing, while Silver smoked a cigarette.

After a time the stallion went off to graze again, while Silver waited through the hot hours. For once in his life he had no plan beyond that waiting.

A glad man was Jim Silver when, late in the morning, he saw a rider jog toward him across the sands from the direction of the ranch house. He watched the little puffs of dust that squirted out from the feet of the horse as the rider drew nearer. Then he made out the bulky form of none other than Sam Waring, who stopped at a considerable distance and waved a white rag or handkerchief slowly back and forth.

Silver grinned as he watched. He took out a bandanna and waved that in answer. Waring seemed still in doubt, but finally he came on slowly. Twice and again he paused for further thought, but at length he rode straight up to the place where Silver sat on a rock, inhaling the smoke of a cigarette.

The hesitation that had appeared in Waring's actions was not in his speech. He summoned a broad smile and waved his hand at Silver.

"All safe and friendly, brother, eh?" he asked cheerfully.

Silver made a noncommittal gesture.

"It seemed a good time for a little talk," said Waring, "so the boys sent me out to find you. They thought you'd be around this valley, somewhere—and here you are."

"Get off the horse and sit down, Waring," suggested Silver. "You don't look happy there. You're too high in the air."

Waring laughed as he got down to the ground.

"I ain't what I used to be in a saddle," he confessed.

"There was a day when I fitted onto a hoss like a clothespin onto a line. But that day's gone, and now I'm kind of swelled up and wabbling with fat."

He sat down on a rock near Silver, took off his hat, mopped his fleshy brow, and went on:

"I've come to talk about young Farrel, of course."

Silver nodded.

"Being a friend of yours," said Waring, "nacherally you want him out of hock."

Silver nodded again.

"And the fact is," said Waring, that he's been in a good deal of danger."

"Has he?" said Silver.

"There was a time last night," said Waring, "when some of the boys wanted to bump him off before he had a chance to get loose and spread the news around about the way they'd been cutting up. If it hadn't been for me talking on his side, something bad would sure 'a' happened to him."

"Thanks," said Silver. "I was behind a rock near the dynamite sack, Waring, when you were interceding for him. I know the kind things you said."

He looked into the eyes of the fat man, but Waring merely laughed.

"You're a fox, Silver," said he. "A regular silver fox, is what you are, and it would take a brighter man than poor old Sam Waring to put anything over on you. But, all jokes aside, young Danny Farrel is in a heap of hot trouble."

"He is," agreed Silver.

"So doggone much trouble that something had oughta be done about it, and that's why I'm out here to talk to you, Jim!"

"Make your proposition," said Silver.

"It's this way," said Waring. "Everybody knows that Silver ain't the sort of a fellow to turn down a friend.

136

Everybody knows that you're the sort who sticks by a partner to the finish. Well, then, this is what we've got in mind: On the one side there's a few cows. On the other side there's a friend. You can make your choice, and I know what choice you'll make."

"It's this way," said Silver. "If I agree to let you fellows get away with the cattle, you'll let me have young Danny Farrel—and his girl beside him."

"Aw, the girl don't count. We throw her in. Sure, you can have her," said Waring. "You don't think that we'd make trouble for a woman, do you, Jim? Do you think that we're that sort of snake?"

"I think," said Silver, "that you'd throttle a baby in a cradle if you could make a hundred dollars out of it."

"Come, come, come!" protested Waring, holding up a fat, soft hand. "You wouldn't wanta talk rough, Jim, would you? The fact is that you and me have to talk business, and it don't help business along to start calling names. You know that, I suppose?"

"I suppose I do," said Silver. "But I've named the proposition, haven't I?"

"Exactly," said Waring. "We've got your young friend. A fine, manly, honest kid, Silver. As manly and honest as I ever seen. It would do me good to see a kid like that wearing my name, matter of fact. But, when all's said and done, business is business. How does it sound to you?"

Silver rubbed his toe in the dust. "I could spoil your business for you, Waring," said he. "I could get to town and gather in plenty of men in a posse to wreck the job for you before your boys will ever be able to gather those cows out of the stampede."

Waring scowled at him with a sudden loss of his cheerful veneer.

"You've raised hell already," said he. "You've spilled more'n a thousand dollars of good beef out of the cup already. It's lying dead back there in the valley to feed the buzzards, and that's your work. What put it into your head to use dynamite to start the stampede?"

"They laid the dynamite down in front of me," said Silver. "You can't expect me to refuse a gift like that, can you?"

Waring stared.

"And then you rode right in through the bunch and got at the cows. Ferris is laid up bad. He's shot inside the shoulder, and he might not pull through."

"I'm sorry for that," said Silver, frowning.

Sam Waring answered suddenly: "Why lie about it, Silver? You're glad that you nicked one of the boys. It pleases you the same's it would 'a' pleased them to put a slug in you. I ain't wrong about that."

"You are," said Silver. "I've seen men that I'd like to drift some lead into. But I hate to shoot at a man I don't know."

Waring grunted his disbelief as he rolled a cigarette.

"How did you happen to have that dynamite along?" asked Silver.

"Ferris again!" exclaimed Waring. "The fool only got what he deserved. He was on a prospecting trip, him and a mule. We come across him in the hills, and we picked up him and our bad luck and brought 'em both along to help out. A lot of help he was. But come on, Silver. Make your bargain."

"I give up a third of the cattle for the sake of one man?" said Silver.

Waring winced, as though he felt the force of this argument.

"Well," he said, "that's the proposition, and I gotta stick to it."

Suddenly Silver nodded. "I'll make the exchange," he said.

Waring heaved a breath of relief.

"Well," he said, "that's great. I gotta admit that you're a reasonable gent to do business with. Mighty reasonable. We'll just run the cows out of the desert and off the ranch into the hills, and then you can have your partner. You can have him safe and sound."

Silver smiled.

"Hey, what's the matter?" asked Waring.

"You keep him till you've got the cattle where you want 'em, eh?" queried Silver.

"What's the matter with that? Mean that you don't trust us, old son?"

Silver shook his head. "If I let you get the cattle through the hills, you may turn Farrel over to me, but he'll be a dead man when I find him."

"I swear," said Waring, lifting one hand and rolling up his eyes with a solemn shake of his head. "I swear—"

"Don't do it," said Silver. "Take your hand down and don't swear. It doesn't work with me, Waring."

The fat man slowly dropped his hand. A faint stain of red crawled up his throat and over his face. He said nothing.

"I'll have to make another sort of deal," said Silver. "I'll have to have security that you'll turn Farrel over to me if I let the herd go."

"What sort of security?" asked Waring.

"A man for a man. If Delgas or Rutherford will put themselves in my hands, I'll take 'em as bail for Farrel."

"Delgas—Rutherford —you ain't crazy, Silver, are you?" shouted Waring.

"It's the only way I'll talk business," said Silver.

Waring stared at him, started to talk, changed his mind. Then he stood up.

"How long before you expect an answer?" he asked.

"Sunset," said Silver. "If one of 'em rides out from the house at sunset, I'll know that he's come to be bail for Farrel, and the deal goes through."

Waring, his head fallen in thought, rode off without another word.

CHAPTER XXI
TRAPPED

Silver waited out the hours of that long afternoon among the sun-baked hills. He was very hungry, and a big jack rabbit obligingly poked its foolish head up above a rock to make a dinner for him. He took off the head of the rabbit with a .45-caliber slug and broiled the flesh over a small fire. He ate it slowly, because he had very little water to wash it down. Parade was now so thirsty that he had stopped grazing altogether, so Silver took him across country to the verge of the big tank and let him drink from that muddy water.

In the sunset he came back toward the ranch house and stopped five hundred yards from it, where he began to drift the horse forward and backward. Nearer he dared not come, for there were men in that outfit to whom even five hundred yards was not impossible with their favorite rifle. He depended on the flare and uncertainty of the light at this time of the day.

In the meantime, he scanned the horizon and saw from south and east and west approaching clouds of dust which told him that some of the punchers were bringing up the cattle that they had collected across the face of the desert. All of those dust clouds moved toward the ranch house as a focus. Some time during the night, perhaps, the big herd would be assembled, and the drift toward the mountains would start.

Already it was rather late. He had waited long, and, if he rode to get help, they might have most of the cattle deep in the ravines before he returned.

He had thought of that all during the day, but he had not dared to ride for a posse. By that means he would be able to save the herd, of course, but he would never be able to save Danny Farrel. They would shoot him out of hand at the first sign of approaching danger, of course.

But what a quandary Delgas and the great Rutherford must be in at this moment, risking, as they were, the value of both land and cattle. For, though they might rush the cows through, they would certainly lose their landed acres as men outlawed for their crime.

It could only be that they hoped against hope that they would be able to sell the herd and deliver it, and then that they could dispose of Farrel and leave Silver with empty hands.

If afterward Jim Silver appeared in the law courts— though that was not his wont—then a staunch agreement between themselves would swear down his testimony in nearly any court of the law.

He thought of this grimly, as he saw the sun go down beneath the horizon without sign of anyone coming toward him from the ranch house.

A number of the punchers had gathered near the house, staring out toward the shimmering, golden figure of the stallion. Silver could see them watching, pointing, gesticulating. He could hear the dim tremors of their voices. He could hear a man calling from the bunk house, a sound like a bird in the far-away sky. But increasing dimness of the twilight thickened the air. And at last, as only a dull band of orange burned along the horizon, he knew that no one would come out to him.

The house disappeared in darkness, then was marked by a single ray of yellow light, which told him of poor Esther at work in her kitchen with ice in her heart.

He looked around the black immensity of the earth, and it seemed to him that his mind was as empty of all resources as the darkening vault of the sky. Still he could hear voices, the slamming of doors, from the house, though he could no longer make out individual figures. But some of the men were probably still there, staring across the night at him, wondering what he, poor fool, could do about it.

That was the thing. What *could* he do?

He could only grit his teeth and pray for an idea. So long as they held poor Danny Farrel, they held Jim Silver, also, and they were clever enough to know this. That was what forced him to make up his mind to the impossible. He would go straight into the house of the enemy and there do what he could for Farrel.

He rode back through the night slowly, trying to sketch a plan. The house was fairly well in his mind, but now he wished that he had drawn a print of every room and every window. He had to plan, and yet there was not much to plan about. It seemed almost better to advance blindly and leave everything to chance when he came in contact with the Rutherford and Waring men.

What worried him most of all was Rutherford. The others might be surprised, taken off their feet by a sudden move; but the imagination of Rutherford was of the capacious sort which understands what other men are likely to conceive.

The shallow draw which ran out of the desert toward the house gave Silver such good cover that he could ride the gold stallion within a very short distance of the place. There he dismounted, made the tall horse lie down, and prepared to go ahead on foot.

He turned himself into a ragamuffin for the purpose. Coat, sombrero, boots, socks went into the discard. He rolled his riding trousers to the knee. He had with him the weight of his two Colts, and that was all, when he came over the edge of the draw and started for the house.

The windmill offered some sort of cover for his advance, but it was the sort of skeleton protection which would be watched by the men on guard without actually making a shield for a spy. So he gave up the thought of the windmill and went straight at the house. He had on the straight line only the almost imperceptible undulations of the ground and one good-sized cactus. It was not protection. It was hardly a hint at protection. What he would have to rely upon was the fact that people do not look for men working like snakes in the dust, as he was working now.

He was almost at the cactus, blessing the size of its three large leaves, when lantern light began to wash across the black earth around him. Not one, but several lanterns were brought, and, while he lay there behind the wretchedly imperfect shadow of that cactus, he saw a lantern nailed up at every corner of the house!

That was Rutherford. He was the fellow who would think of bathing the house with light to expose all who approached, whereas most people would have kept their eyes open in darkness and so would have hoped to trap the invader. But Rutherford had a brain.

Not only was there a light at each corner of the irregular building, but there appeared to be a man on guard there, also.

Silver lay sweating in the dust, and it was by no means the heat of the ground that caused the water to pour.

For his position seemed to him most perfectly helpless. To worm his way forward in the darkness had been dangerous and hard enough. To worm his way backward through the light until he reached the edge of the draw would be worse than madness, he was certain. Then what remained for him to do?

144

In his excitement, he drew a breath that was chiefly dust, and had to lie, strangling, choking, stifling, for whole minutes, controlling the convulsions of his body with a mighty effort of the will to keep from drawing a single gasping breath.

When at last he was able to breathe again, he could give his mind to an insoluble problem. He was more and more convinced that he was hopelessly trapped. There was not even a thing to hope for, except a rain and hail-storm so tremendous that it would blot out the light of the lanterns and give him a chance to crawl away through the mud, but to pray for rain under the starry sky of the desert was like praying for a miracle. Ten months might pass, here, before so much as a shower fell.

The Rutherford men were ideally placed. They had light by which to spy him out if he so much as stirred, and they had their saddle horses at hand if the least suspicious sign appeared to their eyes. They could be in the saddle and away like bullets at the first signal. The mustangs, with thrown reins to anchor them, stood in three groups near the house, four or five in a bunch. There were more than were needed, for the reason, perhaps, that Rutherford had decided to be forehanded and equipped in every possible particular.

Silver, lying flat on his face, could have groaned with despair. He heard one of the men at the nearer corners of the house saying:

"One way of looking at it, this here is a funny busi-ness—we hang out a light for a gent to shoot at us by."

"He won't shoot," said the other. "Silver ain't that kind. There ain't no Injun about him. He don't take no advantages."

"Ain't he a gunman?" asked the other.

"Sure, he's a gunman."

"Then what you mean he don't take advantages? He's

145

faster with a gun than other folks are, and he's straighter with his shooting. That means that he's got all kind of advantages."

"I mean, he don't play 'em. When they crowd him, he fights back, and that's all there is to it."

"You sound kind of nutty to me," said the other. "Here's a gent with a list of dead as long as my arm, and you say he don't take advantages? How could he have such a record if he didn't go out for scalps?"

"You dunno the kind of a fool this bird is. He goes where the water is likely to have fish in it, and then he waits for a fish to show. He don't drop a line in. He waits for the fish to bite him, and then he bites back."

"That sounds like fool talk."

"Does it? What I mean is that he waits for the other gents to crowd him. If they won't crowd him man by man, they'll crowd him in couples or gangs. There ain't many stories of Silver hunted by single men. There's plenty of stories of him hunted by a whole crew."

"It looks to me as though Rutherford and Delgas and Waring have got him beat to a frazzle in this here business."

"Nobody's got him beat till he's ten feet buried underground, and even then he's likely to claw his way out. But there's numbers and brains against him now. There's Waring and Rutherford, to say nothin' of Delgas, that's worth a little speech all by himself."

"What is goin' to happen to Danny Farrel?"

"The same as always happens to a gent that tries to go straight when going crooked is the way the others around him are walking."

A shadow fell over Silver as he listened to the last words. That shadow struck his brain like a bullet. He hardly dared to look up, but then he saw that it was only one of the horses which had edged close to smell at the tempting green and the bristling thorns of the big cactus.

146

If the brute suddenly took notice of a man lying on the ground and jumped away with a snort, it was apt to bring the attention of the guards to Silver.

Then he saw that the thing might be a sort of act of Providence to give him deliverance from his danger of the moment.

Some one called out at the other end of the house. One of the nearest sentries turned to watch; the other sang out in reply.

That moment Silver used to rise slowly to his feet.

He could not sit in the saddle, of course, but he fitted his knee into the stirrup leather just above the stirrup, and, with his weight resting on that support, he slid the other leg far back, hooking his toes around the pony's quarter. With his hands he gripped the saddle flaps. He was embarked. Neither his feet nor his body showed, for the moment. He was something suspended in empty air, as it were.

CHAPTER XXII
IN THE HOUSE

The great advantage was that Silver was at last off the ground. The black shadow of the body of the horse was as a blessing to him, but that mustang was not bestowing more than one blessing at a time. He reached around, got a good grip, and took a bite at the shoulder of Jim Silver. The tough flesh slipped from under the teeth of the horse, but it was agony for Silver. He dared not move to beat the head of the horse away, at that moment, for his knee threatened to slip out of the stirrup leather and let him down with a crash in the dust.

Having taken one nip, the horse seemed content. It began to drift on away from the cactus, moving with very short steps. And Silver discovered that the brute was moving not away from the house but toward it!

It seemed to be trying to steal away from the other animals, by the shortness of its steps deceiving the eyes of the men who watched it.

One of them sang out, "What's the matter with that fool of a hoss?"

"That's Jerry's hoss. He's gone and cinched it up loose. Look at the way that saddle's turned over!"

"I better fix it. If that hoss has to be used, it's gotta be used fast and used hard."

Steps came toward Jim Silver. He loosened the grip

of his right hand, though thereby he made his hold on the horse very precarious.

"Wait a minute. Let Jerry do his own work. He's always sliding out from trouble," said the other sentry.

The footfall paused.

"Yeah, maybe you're right," said the second speaker, and turned back.

"I never seen a freckle-nosed son that was any good, anyway," said the other. "And Jerry's all over freckles."

"He's a lazy hobo," said the other sentry.

Silver, using his right hand to pluck at the mane of the mustang, tried to pull it away from the house and turn the head of the horse in another direction. But the mustang was perceptibly braced against this weight which lay along its side and therefore it naturally moved in the opposite direction. That happened to be toward the house, and nothing that Silver could do would make the pony change his mind. He dared not reach for the reins, of course.

They were now steering past the corner of the house.

"That hoss is sure a drifter," said one of the watchers. "He sure aims to stir around."

"It's Jerry own fault," said the other. "He oughta train a hoss to stand when the reins are once throwed on it."

"Yeah, he'd oughta do that. I wonder is Delgas socking that old rye on the nose, right now?"

By this time the mustang had gone past the corner of the house. As it moved in closer to the wall, a new danger came to Silver, which was that he might now be seen by either of the guards if they chanced to make a single pace out from the wall. But now they were right beside the wall.

Silver softly dropped his feet to the ground, ducked under the neck of the mustang, and stood in front of the black, square mouth of an open window. The blaze of the lanterns struck full on him. He saw the guard off at the right, turn his head and apparently look straight at him. Yet the man in a moment turned his head once more and looked straight before him, whistling! He had seen nothing because he expected to see nothing.

Silver, the next instant, was through the black of the window and kneeling in safety on the floor of the room inside.

Safety? He could hardly call it safety to be in a house where every hand was against him, and where no hands were weak. He heard, very distinctly, the deep voice of Delgas, which was booming in another portion of the house. What a windfall it would be to Delgas and Rutherford if they could get their hands on him!

He smiled a little, as he thought of that.

Then, just outside the window, he heard a voice exclaim: "Look here! Here's a footmark in the dust. Look at it. Right where the mustang was standin'!"

Silver moved like a snake into a corner of the room and lay still.

"Yeah," said the second sentry, joining his companion. "It looks like a footprint, all right."

Then a silence followed in which the imagination of Silver conceived of the truth entering the brains of those fellows.

But presently one of them said: "Well, there ain't any footmarks leadin' up to it. You can see that for yourself."

"Sure I can. But I wanta know how this here mark came."

"I dunno. Maybe it dropped down out of the sky."

"Don't talk like a fool. There ain't anybody around this house that'd be likely to go without boots, is there?"

"Well, how would a mark like that come there? You think that Silver made it?"

"I dunno. I ain't thinking."

"I reckon you ain't, Slim."

"All I know is that it's a funny thing that that mark's on the ground. I dunno what to make of it."

"Maybe an angel made it. Jumped down out of the sky and stamped on the ground, and jumped up into the sky ag'in. Maybe there's an angel laughin' at us right now."

"Aw," said Slim gruffly, "shut up, will you?"

His voice entered the room, as he spoke, and now he scratched a match. Silver, curled up in a corner behind a chair, covered his man with a Colt and prayed that he would not have to shoot.

The flame of the match revealed a long, sallow, evil face, and a gaunt neck with an Adam's apple that moved up and down like a fist.

Slim presently tossed the match over his shoulder and straightened.

"I was just thinking," he said.

"That's likely to be kind of hard on you," said the other.

"Leave me be," said Slim. "I'm goin' to go and report this here."

"Are you? You'll catch it if you do. There's some of the boys that think you ain't too bright already, Slim, and if you start in talkin' about angels that leave their footprints on the ground—well, there'll be trouble!"

"Hold your trap," said Slim, "or I'll slam it shut for you. I'm goin' to tell Rutherford and see what he'll have to say."

The footfall departed with a soft jingling of spurs.

Silver looked desperately about him in the dark of the room. He could not stay there. Where *could* he stay in the place when once the word was brought to the great Rutherford? The active wit of that man would not fail to hitch importance to the mystery of that footprint in the dust.

Silver found the knob of a door and opened it upon

151

the dark of a hall. Through the darkness, voices came to him intimately, dwelling in his ear. He saw the long yellow-red slit of lamplight that showed where a door fitted poorly to its jamb.

Then, in farther distance, he could make out the sharp, high-pitched voice of Slim saying words which he did not understand, but which were undoubtedly about the mystery of that footprint. A moment later the house would be searched. There would be nothing for him except to fight as well as he could until they decided to burn him out. It would not take them very long to decide that, of course.

Another door, just a step down the hallway, yawned suddenly with a low groan of hinges. As he jerked back his head, he saw a lamp carried in the hand of Esther Maxwell, its light close to her tired face and the red blotches of her eyes.

He drew back from her sight still farther, but he called softly out of the darkness of his room, as the light walked toward him in regular pulsations down the hall.

"Esther! Esther! Do you hear me? It's Jim Silver."

He heard the catch and the long take of her breath, like a soft moan. Then he ventured to step out before her. The lamp wobbled out of her hand. He caught it. He took her by the wrists and crushed them together.

"Take hold of yourself!" said Silver savagely.

She nodded, breathless.

"They'll be hunting for me through the house in another minute," said he, returning the lamp to her hand. "Hide me somewhere. In your room is as good as the next place."

He heard the voice of Rutherford calling: "Billy! Mike! Whisky Joe!"

"Quick! Quick!" he urged her.

She tried to run past him up the stairs to show the way, but he checked her. Whatever happened, no run-

152

ning footfalls must be heard by those who would soon be hunting through the place for him.

They went up the narrow stairway. It had no railing for safety or comfort and it was simply bracketed out from the wall, so that squeaking was unavoidable even when he walked close to the supporting wall.

There was no hallway, only a single landing and door at the head of the steps. He opened that and glided through in the lead as a trampling of many feet came into the hall beneath and the voice of Delgas boomed:

"Who's that?"

"It's I," said the girl. "What's wrong?"

Delgas imitated her stammering voice and roared with laughter.

"The little fool's goin' to fall down on her bean," said Delgas. "She's scared pink and blue, already. Well, honey, there ain't nothing wrong—yet—but if there turns out to be a man in the house, there's goin' to be a whole lot wrong. Come on, boys!"

The girl entered the room behind Silver and closed the door behind her, the light staggering in her frightened hand. She turned and looked with ghostly eyes at him.

"What can we do?" said her soundless lips.

He went across the floor like a cat, took the lamp, and put it on the center table.

Then he looked around him.

For a window there was only a pair of square holes punched into the roof, each about a foot wide. The furniture consisted of a small wardrobe, the little center table, the washstand, two narrow chairs, and an iron bedstead. There was no paint on the floor, walls, or ceiling. It was simply a bare box. The air was hot. The sun of the long afternoon had turned the room into an oven. And as the sweat trickled down the face of Silver, seeing how perfectly he was trapped, he thought once

153

more of dead Steve Wycombe who was reaching so strongly out of the grave to draw down after him the man who had taken his life.

Then Silver turned back to the white, staring face of the girl.

"There's nothing for me to do but hide," he whispered. "There's no place for me to hide except under that bed. You do something. Sit down and write a letter. Do anything to show that you're occupied, and if they want to come in to search—don't oppose them!"

CHAPTER XXIII
THE SEARCH

He slid under the bed. It was sufficiently wide and the shadow the lamp threw was sufficiently steep so that he would be hidden from the gaze of any except a man who leaned over and peered for him. But if they searched in the room at all, were they not sure to look carefully under the bed?

He could see the girl sitting at the center table. He could see her as far as her elbows; he could hear the rapid scratching of her pen.

"Where's Danny?" he whispered.

"Don't talk!" she gasped.

"They can't hear, if you whisper. Where's Danny?"

"In your room. With Mr. Rutherford."

"What are they going to do with him?"

"Keep him. They're going to keep him to make sure that you do nothing and then—"

Even her whisper was more than she could maintain, at that point.

And Silver understood. They would keep Dan Farrel with them until the drive into the mountains had been completed and then, instead of giving him freedom, they would put a bullet through his head and leave him for the buzzards and coyotes. They would be reasonably sure that Jim Silver would not interfere so long as his friend was in their hands. It seemed to Silver, as he lay there and ran his swift eye back over the pages of his life, that all his troubles had sprung from his friendships, and yet all of those labors had not yielded him a single friend whom he cared to take with him on his adventures. Where he met a man, there he left him. His partners remained where he had found them, fixed in his memory like the mountains; only Silver went on.

He heard the girl say: "I know what you've done, and no man ever did more for a friend. I've prayed for you when I prayed for Danny."

"Hush!" breathed Silver, as he heard a footfall coming up the stairs.

It was a heavy step, stamping down on the boards, making the flimsy wood groan and squeak under the pressure.

Delgas beat once on the door, heavily, and then flung it open.

"Hello. What's in here?" he roared.

He came thumping into the room with the jingle of the spurs at his heels. The reek of his cigar was instantly in every corner.

"Just takin' a quiet little minute by yourself, eh?" said Delgas to the girl. "You ain't seen nothing of a long streak of poison called Jim Silver, have you?"

She said nothing. She must have been shaking her head.

"Scared stiff, eh?" said Delgas. "So doggone scared that she dunno what to do about it? Can't talk? Just stand there and wag your head? Well, I guess he ain't in here, unless he's under the bed."

The big feet of Delgas crossed the room, and he kicked at the empty space under the bed. That maneuver came so unexpectedly that Silver barely flinched his face back in time enough to escape from catching the blow.

Delgas turned again.

"There ain't anything for you to be so shakin' about,"

156

said Delgas. "He can't do you no harm, this gent Silver. Not while gents like me are around. You know why? Because I'd take care of you. You're an uncommon pretty girl, Esther, and I been noticin' you. You'd be a help to a gent. There's only one funny thing about you, and that's why you cotton to a doggone common gent like poor Danny Farrel. I'll tell you why. It's because there ain't anything to a feller like that. There ain't any sand to him, and there ain't any brains. He's in the soup, and the best way for you is to forget him and take a look around for something else in the way of a man. And when you're lookin', stop your eye a minute on Morrie Delgas. He ain't pretty, but he's got a silver lining!"

When he finished, he broke into a great, bawling laughter that filled the room and half deafened Silver. Then, still braying, Delgas went out of the room and creaking down the stairs, slamming the door behind him.

Through the flimsy partitions, Silver could hear Delgas saying: "No sign of him up there. No sign of nobody. It ain't likely he'd be fool enough to come into this house anyway, is it?"

"When you know enough," answered the voice of Rutherford, "to read the mind of Jim Silver and say what he's likely to do and what he's not likely to do, I'll take my hat off to you and go to work for you, Morrie. You weren't long enough in that room to search it."

"That's a lie," answered Delgas. "I was long enough to search the room and kiss the girl and come back again."

And the long uproar of his laughter went quivering through the house once more.

"Steady, now!" whispered Silver. "That's Rutherford coming, and he's twice the danger that's in Delgas."

There was a polite rap at the door.

"Come in!" called the girl.

The door opened.

"Sorry to bother you, Esther," said Rutherford, "but I ought to glance over this room. Delgas is a little careless."

"I've been right here," said the girl.

"He was in the house before you went up to your room," answered Rutherford.

He paused.

"I don't see where he *could* be, though," said Rutherford.

There was another pause.

Then he asked: "Writing letters through all the excitement, Esther?"

"I had to do something," said the girl. "I've been half hysterical. *Is* Jim Silver in the house?"

"Excuse me a moment," said Rutherford. "I hate to do this, but little things are sometimes important."

Paper rustled. He read:

> "DEAREST MOTHER: It's high time that I should write you a letter because I haven't written for a long time and if—"

There was another pause.

"Yes," said Rutherford quietly. "I should say that you *have* been half hysterical—or else that you were simply scratching words down on paper for the sake of seeming occupied. It isn't that, my dear, is it?"

"*Seeming* occupied?" the girl stammered.

"There's nothing but the bed that could hide anything," said he.

And he walked straight toward it.

Silver hesitated a tenth part of a second. He could kill Rutherford, easily enough, but the report of the gun would bring the others, and nothing in the world could save him then.

He hooked his toes inside the cross rod at the head

158

of the bed; he grasped the cross rod at the foot of the bed; and in that manner he was able, with a great effort, to heave himself up until his back touched the springs.

He saw the slender, pointed toes of the boots of the great Rutherford approach, shining like quicksilver. The boots paused. There was the deadly gleam of a Colt six-gun beneath the hanging edge of the coverlet. Then he saw the shadow of Rutherford sweep over the floor as he bent down.

He tensed himself to receive the shock of the bullet.

Instead, Rutherford straightened again, and walked back across the room.

"Well," said he, "I'm sorry that I've bothered you, Esther. In a time like this, with a fellow such as Silver in the offing, I have to take precautions. You understand that?"

She failed to answer. And he laughed as he said:

"You look as though a glance under your bed was worse than murder, my dear."

He went out; the door closed; and Silver relaxed once more on the floor beneath the bed.

He could not believe his escape. His brain was still spinning with the sensation of imminent death, as he watched the feet of the girl go stumbling to a chair into which she fell.

He whispered. There was no answer for a long moment.

Then, very dimly, from the outside of the house he heard a man exclaiming: "He's a regular Robinson Crusoe, old Slim is. He seen a footprint in the dust and he went and raised hell about it, was what he did. Good old Slim, he's the kind of a gent that don't let none of the small change slip."

There was laughter, after this, and then the small voice of the girl close to Silver murmured:

"We're saved, Jim Silver."

Silver slid out from beneath the bed and got to his feet.

"You'll be safe here," she said. Her face was shining. "And in the morning when they start the herd, you can get out of the house with no trouble at all."

Out of the distance, as though fulfilling a part of her words, he heard the bawling of cattle.

"And Danny?" he asked her.

The joy was struck out of her face. But she shook her head, answering: "You've tried to do more than any other man in the world would try. You can't do more. You've got to hide and be quiet."

He looked at the narrow windows.

There was no way through them, of course. There was no possible exit from the room except down the narrow, squeaking stairway. But he was determined, in some manner, to get to Danny Farrel on this night.

"There's nothing more you can do," whispered the girl urgently. "Don't try anything."

"I've got to think," said Silver.

He sat down in a chair, made a cigarette, remembered himself, and dropped the makings of it into his pocket. There was a wall of darkness before his brain, and it would not lift.

He looked at the girl.

She had grown older. She had been very pretty, before, but she was almost ugly, now, to the eye. What she had gained for Silver was a touch of inward beauty. If she were doddering in wrinkled age, she would never be less than beautiful to him, knowing what he knew of her.

And he whispered to her suddenly: "I think that I'll have luck. I don't know how. But I think that I'll have luck."

One of the cow-punchers on guard outside the house began to sing loudly. Another sentinel exclaimed:

160

"Shut up! Don'tcha know some of the boys are tryin' to get a wink of sleep now?"

Silver stood up from the chair. He took the hand of the girl in silence.

"Don't make a noise," he told her. "I understand what I'm about. Nobody can do anything without luck, anyway, and I'm just going to ask for an extra slice of luck now."

Then he opened the door and looked down into the black well of the hallway.

CHAPTER XXIV

RUTHERFORD'S OPINION

The girl came after him. She dared not so much as whisper, now that the door of her room was open, but she grasped his arm with both hands.

He removed her grip and closed the door in her face. Then he lay down on his side, close to the wall, and began to work his way down the stairs, feet first. In that way, his weight was distributed over a number of the steps. He was close to the wall where his poundage would exercise the least leverage on the supporting brackets. And so, inch by inch, he wormed his way down toward the hall below.

He was nearly to the bottom when a door swung open, a broad flash of light entered the hall and streamed into the eyes of Silver. On the threshold stood Red, the light glancing through his tousled hair. After a moment he closed the door softly.

What had he heard to bring him there? What had he seen when he looked through?

Silver, standing now on the floor of the hall with a gun in each hand, waited breathlessly, but he heard no alarm given, no lifting of voices, no scurrying of quick feet. Red, it seemed, had seen nothing. Once more it was proved that a man sees only what he expects to see, and a man prone on the stairs was not what a man expects to see.

162

Silver went to the door of that room which he had used for lounging while he was in the house. The voices inside were those of Waring, Delgas, Rutherford, and young Danny Farrel.

They were still talking about the print of the naked foot, with Waring saying:

"The way I aim to live, gents, I don't get no dyspepsia about things that don't bother me none and ain't in my way. If there was ten thousand footprints in the dust and a chance to grab ten bucks off a table, I'd take the ten bucks and let the ten thousand footprints go."

Delgas laughed at this viewpoint, heartily.

"I say the same," said he.

"Look here, Farrel," said Rutherford. "You're a lad with a brain. Whatever you think, you can't help your partner, Silver. Suppose you tell me what you think made that footprint."

"One of your own men trying to string the rest of you along," said Farrel instantly.

"You're all against me then," answered Rutherford. "And I'll tell you what *I* think."

"Blaze away," said Delgas.

"I think," said Rutherford, "that Jim Silver made the mark."

"Hey!" said Delgas. "Watcha mean, Harry? You mean that Jim Silver's been that close to the house and not come inside? What kind of reason have you got for it, anyway?"

"I know something about Silver," said Rutherford. "I have to study fellows like that. And it's an old saying with every man West of the Mississippi who has to live by his wits that it's better to have a sheriff and his posse after you than it is to have Jim Silver on your trail. I've thought that I'd always be clever enough to keep out of his way—but this time he's after me!"

"You don't like it, Harry, do you?" asked Waring.

"I hate it like the devil," answered Rutherford frankly.

"Got the wind up?" asked Waring, chuckling.

"I have," said Rutherford. "So would the rest of you, if you had any sense."

"Go on, brother, and clear that up for us," suggested Delgas. "Why ain't we got any sense?"

"Because if you knew Silver, you'd be as sure as I am that he left that footprint behind him."

"Go on and open up," urged Waring.

"Silver's like a sailor," said Rutherford. "When there's dangerous work ahead, he likes to go at it with bare feet. Bare feet are the best on a slippery deck. They're more silent than shoes, too."

"They ain't so good in a fire." Waring chuckled.

"Silver's are," said Rutherford.

"Wait a minute," broke in Delgas. "You mean, Harry, that Silver has the habit of going around in bare feet when he's about to raise the devil?"

"If he's going to enter a house where he wants to be as quiet as a moving shadow—yes, he'd be in bare feet."

"But he's not in the house, Harry."

"That's what you say."

"Why, man," said Waring, "ain't we looked the place over from head to heel? We ain't seen a thing!"

"Not a thing," echoed Delgas. "Not a thing, and I looked over every inch of the house myself."

"Nobody has seen anything," answered Rutherford. "Nobody saw a man come up to the house. There were four guards out there and plenty of lantern light. But one minute that dust was clear, except for horse tracks, and the next minute, there's the print of a naked foot. Do you think it was a ghost that made the mark, Delgas?"

"I dunno," said Delgas. "It beats me, is what it does."

"Somebody came up to this house and made that mark before he got through the window—or climbed up to the roof!

164

"Aye, the roof!" cried Delgas. "I never thought of that!"

"I did, though," said Rutherford. "I thought of the roof and ran a ladder up and climbed up to the top, but there's nothing to see on the top of the house."

"He's not on the roof, and he's not in the house. And if he came up and made his mark in the dust, then he went off again the same way he came," said Delgas. "That's the long and the short of it."

"It's the long of it and the wrong of it," answered Rutherford. "A fellow like Silver went through a lot of danger to get that close to the house, and he wouldn't turn away again before he'd accomplished something. You fellows ought to see that."

"I don't get what you're drivin' at. You have me beat," said Waring. "It kind of sounds like geometry to me, and I never was no good in funny things like that."

"Well," said Delgas, "let Harry blaze away and tell us what's what. He'll be talkin' about ghosts walkin', before long. Even Harry can be wrong, I guess."

"You think that Silver is a ghost?" asked Rutherford.

"I don't say that I think that," answered Delgas.

"Well," said Rutherford, "I can't tell you any more reasons, unless you count the feeling in my marrow bones as a reason, but I'll tell you that I'm sure that Jim Silver is in this house at this moment!"

"Hi!" yelled Waring.

Somebody started up out of a chair and crossed the room with heavy steps and stood at the door.

"You mean that, Harry?" said Delgas. "What makes you say so?"

"I've told you my reasons, and you say they're no good. I say that Jim Silver made that print in the dust, and that Jim Silver made that print just before he slipped through the open window into the house. We searched the place and we couldn't find him, any more than our guards outside were able to see him walk right up to the house through the lantern light. But in spite of that, he's somewhere in this house."

"Where?" shouted Delgas.

"I don't know. Outside that door, perhaps—from the feeling that's inside my spine!" said Rutherford.

"Doggone if it don't begin to scare me—it's a regular ghost story!" exclaimed Waring. "It makes me sweat, though I feel pretty cold. Is that fellow in on it? Farrel, have you got a hand in this?"

"How could he have a hand in it?" asked Delgas. "Waring, you're nutty."

"What Harry says is enough to make any man nutty," cried Waring. "We been over this place with a fine-toothed comb, and now we start in talkin' about ghosts. I ain't no hero even when it comes to fightin' men, and I lay off when it comes to ghosts. I don't want no part of 'em!"

"If you got this idea in your head," said Delgas, "what you want us to do about it, Harry?"

"I don't know," said Rutherford. "We've got the house guarded. There's nobody asleep except in the bunk house, and they're ready to turn out and ride at any minute. I don't very well know what more we can do."

"Except to keep our eyes open," suggested Delgas.

"That's it," said Rutherford. "We've got to keep on the alert, my friends."

"It makes me nervous, though," said Waring. "Delgas, get away from that door. You act like you was afraid that somebody would walk in through it. If Jim Silver can do what you gents say, he don't need to open the door. He'll slide in through the keyhole, and turn out of a mist into a man, like they do in the fairy tales."

"Yeah?" said Delgas. "I dunno."

The door jerked open so rapidly that the gesture was almost too fast for Jim Silver, even. He had barely time to snatch out a revolver as the door pulled wide and Delgas stood scowling on the threshold.

Silver beat the heavy butt of a revolver into the center of that scowl. As Delgas fell senseless on his back, Silver stepped over the body and took the remaining pair under the muzzles of his guns.

CHAPTER XXV

A BEATEN CREW

Rutherford's first gesture was a flick of the fingers that nearly touched the handles of his gun beneath his coat. But his thought was faster still. It saw that he was well-covered, and his second thought brought the hand away again. He sat leaning forward a little in his chair, looking not at the leveled Colt but into the steady, gleaming eyes of Silver. They were worth seeing. A changing yellow light glowed and sank and rose again in them.

Big Waring had got his hand as far as the gun on his hip, and there his grasp froze.

It was strange that a face could change so suddenly. All his jowls and the hanging flap of the flesh beneath his chin were struck stone-white, and all about his mouth was white, too. His upper lip began to work. And his great red nose stood out like a thing painted with blood, and his eyes were as bright as the eyes of a hawk. One could tell by the look of them that the spirit in the man was greater than any professions he made of courage. Whatever his faults were, he was a fighting machine.

"Here we are again," said Silver.

He kicked the door shut behind him.

"Stand up and come over here, Danny," he commanded.

Farrel rose. He was shaking from head to foot. He

168

was the only man in the room who seemed close to a break-down.

"Don't get between me and either of them," said Silver.

Farrel edged around the wall as though a great fire were blazing in the center of the room. He had to take short steps because of the rope that was fastened about his knees. His hands were tied behind his back.

"You two," said Silver, "turn and face the wall."

He added: "Hoist your hands, first. And see that the hand you lift from that hip is empty, Waring. I'm watching you a little harder than I'm watching Rutherford, in case you're in doubt about it."

Starting to turn, Waring and Rutherford looked at one another. They paused and seemed to consult with glances. Then they kept on turning until they were facing the wall. They lifted their hands high above their heads and stood rigid. The tail of Waring's coat was hitched up almost to the small of his back, and his big-handled revolver showed.

Silver said: "I'm going to shift one gun into my pocket and keep you fellows covered with the right-hand gun only. If you want to try a sudden break, that'll be your opportunity."

He slipped one gun down between his legs, as he spoke. A shudder went through the body of Waring. Rutherford, who seemed to read the mind of his companion, barked suddenly:

"Don't be a fool, Waring. You'll get the pair of us killed out of hand, the first thing you know."

So Waring stood fast, but the noise of his heavy breathing was loud through the room.

Silver took out a knife, pressed the spring that made the blade fly out, and, without taking his eyes from his double target, found the ropes that tied the hands of Dan Farrel.

When Farrel was free, he snatched the knife from Silver, cut the tie rope that bound his knees together, and leaned over Delgas.

"This fellow first, Jim?" he asked.

"Take him first," agreed Silver.

He gave one glance downward to the bleeding face of Delgas. It sagged as though the blow on the forehead had smashed all the other bones of the countenance so that the features were as soft as putty.

Farrel threw the man's coat open and took away the guns from the holsters beneath the pits of the arms. He took a bit of the rope which had been used on him and trussed Delgas hand and foot. The fallen man was coming to. He breathed like one out of breath after being in water, making a heavy puffing sound.

Still his eyes were not open when Farrel left him and went across the room to the other pair. They had not stirred. Only, as the shadow of Farrel swept across the wall, Waring said half aloud:

"Somebody gets it, for this."

His big, fat body was still quivering. His pretended humility left him. He was the fighting beast pure and simple, overlaid with certain layers of blubber.

Farrel got the guns, and from Waring a long, straight-bladed knife that could apparently be used for throwing as well as for handwork.

After that, he procured more rope and made the two fast. He had finished that task and armed himself with a pair of guns when the voice of Red came down the hallway, softly singing. His hand fell with a respectful knock at the door.

"Come!" called Silver.

The door opened, with the voice of Red coming cheerfully through the gap before the way was clear to his eyes.

"The herds are coming up," he said, "and we're ready to start running 'em at the—"

He had the door open by this time. He could see his three leaders helplessly tied, and the guns of Silver were hardly a yard from his breast. He put out his head in a queer way, like a rooster stretching his neck before crowing. Then he began to hoist his hands. They were level with his shoulders before Silver said:

"You see the lay of the land, brother?"

Red nodded convulsively.

And he whispered immediately afterward, under his breath: "I had the hunch right from the start. I had the hunch that I wouldn't be able to push the thing through. I knew from the start that the crooks would go down— fool that I am!"

"Jim, don't do him any harm," said Danny Farrel.

He moved up a hand toward his own bruised face.

"Except for Red, I'd have every bone in my body broken," said Farrel. "I'd be dead by this time, I guess, or worse than dead, if Delgas had had his way with me, but Red stood in between."

"Did he?" asked Silver.

His cold eye ran slowly over the body and then over the face, over the frightened, staring soul of the cowpuncher.

"Talk up for yourself, Red," said Silver. "Any reason why you shouldn't go where the other three are going?"

Red started to speak, thought better of it, locked his jaws. He thrust out his head still farther and looked Silver suddenly in the eyes.

"You go to the devil," said Red.

At that, Silver laughed.

"Not going to make any excuses, Red?" he asked.

The thick shoulders of the cow-puncher shrugged.

"Well," said Silver, "I'll tell you what. You just ease

171

yourself outside the door and go tell the other boys that the game's up. We've got the three of 'em. We've got them, but if the rest of the boys want to take their horses and high-tail out of these diggings, nobody will stop 'em. Understand?"

Red nodded.

"Get out!" commanded Silver.

Red hesitated one longer moment. Then he backed through the door with his hands still held high. He kept on backing till the dark of the hall was about to swallow him, and Silver slammed and locked the door in his face.

He turned and sat down.

Delgas woke up with a start and began to babble: "Come on, boys! Come on! Down with 'em!"

"Oh, shut up," said Rutherford. "Don't you know you're licked with the rest of us?"

Delgas sat up, and started at Silver.

"It's no good," he said. "You done some mind reading, Harry—and Silver *was* in the house all the time."

"Sure he was in the house," snarled Rutherford.

Waring sank his big chin on his chest and stared down at the table. His rage had not grown less. When his eyes stirred, they showed smoking fire.

"Beaten," he said, "like three curs."

"It looks to me as though we can send you fellows up for close to life," Silver said. "Cattle rustling doesn't go down very well in this state."

Rutherford was staring at Silver in silence. His eyes could not move from the face of the big man.

But Delgas said: "We'll find our way out of that."

"It looks to me," said Silver, "that we can make some sort of an agreement out of this thing."

He was interrupted by a sudden outburst of yelling from the men beyond the house. Some one fired three shots through the outer wall of the rooms and roared:

"Rutherford! Rutherford! Speak up and let's know the truth about it!"

"Hello!" called Rutherford calmly. "That you, Lefty?"

"It's me, and what—"

"Shut up," said Rutherford.

Lefty was still.

"I'm tied hand and foot," said Rutherford. He took out the words one by one, like a showman exhibiting his wares. The deliberation with which he spoke was apparently a sign of the exquisite agony of shame which he was enduring. He could not grow paler, because his face was normally as pale as a bone, but his mouth kept working slightly at the corners.

"You're tied hand and foot?" howled Lefty. "Where's Delgas then? Is what Red tells us the straight of it?"

"Red tells you the straight," said Rutherford.

A torrent of cursing came from Lefty, who finished: "What's happened?"

"I've been a fool," said Rutherford. "I've been handled like a baby. There's nothing I can do. You boys take care of yourselves, because Jim Silver has won once more!"

Lefty departed. He bade no farewell, but his going was announced by the diminishing volume of his voice as he went off, cursing at every step. A moment later, with a wild whooping, the whole body of the cow-punchers started to circle the house, and the louder they yelled, the faster they fired their revolvers into the building.

Nearly every one of the bullets ranged through the house from side to side. One struck the table and split it clear across. Another peeled a great splinter off the floor, slapping it up against the wall. Another smashed the knob of the door, striking out a chime as if from a bell. Still another slug took the hat off Waring's head.

Danny Farrel shrank into a corner. It was notable that

not one of the other four so much as stirred in his place. Silver occupied himself, during the uproar, with making a cigarette for Delgas. He put it between the lips of Delgas and lighted it. Delgas nodded his thanks as the horde of cow-punchers and ex-convicts ran yelling off across the desert.

"All right," said Silver, "we can talk business now. The boys have gone. Waring, I suppose you're the most poisonous of the gang. We'll take enough of your money to pay for as many steers of mine as are missing, but I don't think we'll take your scalp. Rutherford, you and Delgas have one easy way out. You've tried to do more harm, here, than you've managed to wangle, but—"

A door slammed. The steps and the voice of the girl rapidly approached the room.

Silver's nerves for the first time showed that they were ragged. He jerked a thumb over his shoulder.

"Go and stop that noise!" he commanded Farrel.

Dan Farrel left the room. As he opened the door, Silver could hear the girl crying out in a frenzied panic.

The door shut, and Silver sighed with relief. He found that Waring was looking at him with a queer, twisted smile.

"You don't like the females, Silver, eh?" he asked.

"Maybe not," answered Silver.

"That's a weakness," said Waring. "And I'm glad to know that you've got one. But, believe me, brother, the bigger you are and the longer you take, the harder you'll fall for 'em, one of these days. Go on and talk your business. I've lost a lot on this job, and I'm going to call myself lucky to get out without losing more blood than dollars."

CHAPTER XXVI

THE HAND FROM THE GRAVE

The end of the thing was in sight. Silver was quick about it. He merely said: "Delgas, you and Rutherford got in on this thing for nothing. It was Steve Wycombe's idea to hook the three of us. Well, you almost snagged me, and just slipped up."

"Where were you?" said Delgas.

"Hanging onto the rods under the girl's bed," said Silver, and smiled on them.

They heard in silence. Rutherford swayed his pale face from side to side.

"Yeah," said Delgas. "All the big things come easy."

"Now, then," said Silver, "I've plenty of stuff on you, out of this deal. I can have you sent up. But I'm giving you a break."

"Show me the break, and then I'll believe it," answered Delgas."

"Listen and learn," said Silver calmly. "Delgas, all you need to do is to sign a little paper that I'll draw up for you. That paper deeds your share of the ranch to Danny Farrel. Understand?"

"Hey," said Delgas, "why should I deed my share to that bum. *He* ain't the one that handed me the rap! Deed it to you, you mean?"

"To Farrel," said Silver. "Except for him, the job would never have gone through."

He himself sat down at the table and took pen and paper. Rapidly he wrote, in a hand strangely small and swiftly flowing. When he had ended, he passed the paper to Delgas.

"How does that sound to you?" Silver asked.

"Yeah, I'll sign," said Delgas. "Same for Harry?"

"Ask him," said Silver.

"Same for you, Harry?" asked Delgas.

Rutherford merely smiled. "The big hombre knows me better than I thought," he declared.

"What's that mean?" asked Delgas. "Have I gone and missed anything? I won't sign, then. I ain't signed it yet, anyway."

"You'll sign, you flat-faced fool!" said Rutherford. "I mean, the big boy knows what's in my mind. I don't take anything but lead from him."

Silver opened the door and called. Danny Farrel answered at once with a joyous voice, and the girl's cry of triumph joined with the sound.

"Danny," Silver said, "get a pair of horses. Put Esther on one of 'em, and clear out. Don't come back to this place before morning. Stay five mile away from it, unless you want to take a chance on your hide. Get out fast."

The girl's voice began to protest, but Farrel could be heard to say:

"Whatever he says is good enough for me. Come on. We'll ride when Silver tells us to."

"I dunno what the gag is," said Delgas, agape.

Waring had closed his eyes. The motion of his lower jaw against his chest made his head sway up and down.

"They're going to have it out, first," he said. "They're going to shoot it out, brother. Those two hombres ain't made to live and circulate. Not on one little earth like this. The continents is too frequent, and the oceans is just wet places to step across, for birds like them."

"I guess we can agree, Harry," Silver said.

"I guess we can," said Rutherford. "I'll sign if you'll fight for it afterward, Silver."

"I'll fight for it," said Jim Silver.

He sat down to write, once more, and completed the second paper, by which Mr. Harry Rutherford legally transferred his rights to the Wycombe ranch to Daniel Farrel. When he had ended, he took two revolvers, laid one at each end of the table, and set Rutherford free from the ropes. He kept a gun in his hand until Rutherford had signed his name.

"Funny thing," said Waring, as he looked on. "Now you've done the job for him, he could let the daylight into you, Harry."

"He's an honorable man, though," answered Rutherford. His malice twisted his smile as he flung the pen down on the floor.

"What happens?" he asked.

"Go back to that opposite wall," said Silver.

Rutherford went back to the opposite wall. Silver faced him. The table was exactly between them, and in front of each, a stride away, was a loaded gun.

"Stand a few inches away from the wall," said Silver.

Rutherford obeyed.

"That's to even things up," said Silver. "I'm taller than you are and I could reach farther. Now, Harry, I'll just toss this gun aside, and when I do that, we'll both go for the guns. Is that right?"

"Right!" said Rutherford.

He looked aside at Waring, and then he said: "Silver, killing you is going to be the sweetest thing in my life!" He had put so much passion into the words that his breath was exhausted. He drew it in again with a drinking sound. And his eyes devoured Silver. His head was back. The eyelids were half lowered. He had almost the look of a man staring at a thing of surpassing beauty. There was the same sort of a smile on his face.

"Are you ready?" asked Silver.

"Ready," said Rutherford.

"Are you on edge?"

"On edge!"

"Then go!" said Silver, and threw his gun aside.

He leaped for the other weapon at the same instant, and saw the flash of Rutherford's hand, bright with speed like a bit of metal.

Then, before Silver's eyes, he saw the table heel over and the Colt spill off to the side. It was Waring, who with his long leg had managed to reach the foot of the table and hook it suddenly toward him, spilling both weapons at Rutherford and away from Silver.

He saw Rutherford bending, picking a falling gun out of the air. But Silver did not dodge. He went straight on, and with the lift of his shoulder caught the edge of the table, hurling it before him right at Harry Rutherford.

Catching the gun from the air with unfailing hand, Rutherford had tried a snap shot even before he straightened his body. The bullet slit open the shirt along Silver's left side. Then, with his bulk behind it, the table crashed against Rutherford.

The gun spoke again, but there was no whir of a bullet in the air. Waring was up, kicking at Silver with his spurs, using them as a game-cock fights. But Silver, bare-footed and swift as a cat, was on the other side of the table in an instant and had caught up a fallen Colt—his own. One gesture with that gun sent Waring crowding back into a corner.

Most of the body of Rutherford was hidden under the table, but his head and shoulders, jammed up against the wall, were visible. He had both arms pinned down, and he was not struggling to get free. Something about the eyes of the man told Silver just what had happened.

He jerked the table away and saw on the breast of Rutherford the spreading red stain of the blood. As the table struck him, a bullet from his own gun had penetrated his body. No doctor on earth would be able to heal that wound. Still, with a nerveless hand, he was trying to pick up the fallen revolver from the floor, but the weight of it slid through his fingers.

Rutherford began to smile.

"Poor Steve Wycombe thought he could make it three for one," said he huskily. "But the poor devil was out of luck. He only got an even break. He only got—me!"

He seemed to nod a confirmation of his last words, but Silver knew that the head would never lift again. He picked up the body. It was hardly more heavy than the body of a child. Silver laid it straight on the floor and closed the eyes. He stood up and turned to Waring. Delgas, all this while, had sat entranced. Events had moved a little too fast for his comprehension.

"I ought to put you there beside him on the floor," said Silver to Waring. "But you're a little too old. Besides, I need you for a witness, on both those little documents. But the law will do the rest of the talking to you, partner. You're old enough to need a rest, and the state will take care of you free of charge."

That was how Steve Wycombe finished off his deal. He had, most surely, put a hand from the grave and taken one living man from the face of the earth. Delgas, a discredited man among his own kind, was turned loose; and Waring went up for a long term.

As for Mr. and Mrs. Daniel Farrel, they wanted Jim Silver to stay on with them indefinitely because, as Farrel said, he would never consider that two thirds of the ranch really belonged to him. He was really holding it merely in trust for Silver. They followed Silver as far as the corner of the corral and watched him saddle Parade and mount, and still they poured out arguments.

Silver looked down at them and smiled. He had said good-by before.

"I can't stay," he said. "I'm awash with cash that needs spending. Besides, it's not the sort of a place for me."

"Why not?" asked Farrel. "You stay here for a while, Jim, and you'll love it the way I do. Those three mountains will be like three friendly faces to you, every day of your life. What's wrong?"

"It's the air," said Jim Silver. "There's too much honesty in it, now, and not enough action." He smiled, and added: "You see, when I came here, it was simply as a prospector in a land of trouble, with the chance of a rich strike of danger straight ahead."

"Well, Jim," said Farrel, "you surely made a big strike of what you were looking for. So I suppose you're satisfied."